RU 00
LE

Scl

Baptised in Blood

BAPTISED IN BLOOD

Janie Bolitho

Constable · London

First published in Great Britain 2000
by Constable, an imprint of Constable & Robinson Limited
3 The Lanchesters, 162 Fulham Palace Road
London W6 9ER
Copyright © Janie Bolitho 2000
The right of Janie Bolitho to be identified as the author of
this work has been asserted by her in accordance with
the Copyright, Designs and Patents Act 1988

ISBN 0 094 80480 X

Printed and bound in Great Britain

A CIP catalogue record for this book is available from the
British Library

For Joy Robinson, Linda Campbell and
Sarah Prance of the breast care unit,
Derriford Hospital, Plymouth.

1

Carmen Brockham sat in the shade of the huge oak in the grounds at the back of the house. Skin formed on an untouched cup of tea as she thought about her life and what she had made of it. It had all seemed enough until she met Neil. *If I lose him now none of it will matter; not the business nor the money,* she realised. Never before had she known what it was to love someone. Neil was the first person who had made her want to talk, to confide things she normally kept to herself. In doing so she had discovered a new sense of self-awareness. Only when he had asked her about the store did Carmen realise how fiercely proud of it she had become.

'I rarely need to go in,' she had said. 'Accountants deal with the financial side, the buyers can be trusted not to make mistakes and the staff are excellent, especially my manager, Malcolm.' But she omitted to say that he was one of the reasons her appearances were infrequent. Malcolm had been a part of her life for too many years. He was the one person who could spoil her chance of happiness.

Naturally, being one of the family, now the only survivor, Carmen knew the history of Brockham's. The *Rickenham Herald* had run an article when she had taken control; the cutting now lay in a box with other bits of nostalgia.

'The sign used to be on the brickwork between the second and third floor,' she said. ' "Brockham and Son's Department Store", it used to say. Awfully cumbersome.' Now it was lower and, in looping green neon, it simply read 'Brockham's'. 'My grandfather, Ernest Brockham, purchased it in 1949 when it was a drapers' shop. It was before the end of rationing, but he took a gamble on the future which paid off. Over the next dozen or so years he acquired the properties on either side of it and expanded the business. There was a grand opening, and a photograph of him and the mayor who performed the ceremony actually made the front page of the *Rickenham Herald*,' she'd told Neil. Carmen, when she was going through some old papers, had come across it. 'Anyway, three years later Grandfather dropped dead at the Cheltenham Festival without knowing whether the horse he had backed in the Gold Cup had won or not. A lot of drinking had been done that day so it was some time before anyone realised he was dead. Everyone assumed that, like many others, he was the worse for wear and unable to stand. People just stepped over or around him. It wasn't drink that killed him. He had an enormous appetite and was very overweight. His heart simply gave up.

'Grandfather enjoyed life and its many ironies, he would have been amused by the fact that his son, his only child, also died prematurely – from cirrhosis of the liver. Everyone assumed Grandfather drank too much, but it was his son who was the real drunk. His name was Henry: he was my father.'

'You poor thing,' Neil had said, stroking her hair.

'It's a long time ago now. Anyway, Dad moved with the times and modernised the store, but even so there are still locals who can remember the grinding old lift with its metal trellised gate. It would often stop between floors. Anyone browsing in Linens who happened to look up would be treated to the sight of the passengers' lower limbs. Do you know, it was still there in the late fifties.'

'Go on.' Neil had smiled, fascinated as she spoke.

'Well, until that time all the money was sent to the cashier in the cubicle at the back of the store via an overhead chute constructed of solid brass. Dad said it was polished every day when he was a boy. Change and a handwritten receipt would be sent back to the salesman or woman in the same manner. Of course, almost every transaction was cash in those days.

'He never said, but I'm sure my father must've been disappointed he never had a son. Three months after I was born my mother ran off with a visiting salesman. I never knew her.'

In 1978 Carmen Brockham took over the business. She did not share her forebears' self-indulgent streak but she had not escaped the fatal flaw which spanned the Brockham generations. She lacked security but did not trust anyone to provide her with it, not until she met Neil. Knowing it to be wicked, she half hoped that something would happen to Malcolm, some quick, painless death that would leave her free to marry. But he was lean and fit and showed hardly any signs of ageing and certainly none of retiring.

Before it became hers at the age of twenty-four, Carmen had paid little attention to the running of the store. On her first proper tour, along with the family solicitor and an accountant who could not hide his admiration of her, she took note of everyone and everything. Once more the store had become outdated.

'The whole place needs a refit, the staff look like old crones or over-the-hill butlers, and God knows where the fashion buyer found those sacks of dresses,' she said later, in the lounge bar of the George where the solicitor and the accountant had argued over who was to pay for her drink. 'We're two years away from the eighties. I want the place revamped, not just for the next decade but in readiness for the nineties.'

And in this she had succeeded. There were glass-sided escalators and designer labels as well as more economically priced goods. Many of the staff were pleased to take early retirement, along with a generous cheque. Profits grew annually, as did Carmen's bank balance. The staff were paid well and rewarded not only with a Christmas party and a bonus but also with a midsummer barbecue. And Malcolm, of course, was always present. She could never take Neil to one of these functions, he would be easily recognised and Malcolm would know how to strike.

At the age of forty-six Carmen remained single, partly because she had been unable to choose from the many suitors she still attracted, but mainly because she was wise enough to realise that the main ingredient of marriage was love. Men had loved her but the reverse was not true.

'I feel like a schoolgirl,' she had told her reflection in the mirror the first night Neil had taken her out. She was studying her face for changes, certain she would look different because she felt different. She had known from the start that he was the man she wanted to be with.

Carmen sighed. A paperback lay unopened on her knees. Impossible to read, impossible to concentrate on anything other than Malcolm Graham, the thorn in her side. Staff at Brockham's came and went: he was the one exception. Carmen had appointed him as store manager not long after she had inherited the business. It was time to act. Twenty-one years was long enough to have been in his debt. Carmen refused to think of it as blackmail.

It was Thursday. Neil was not due back until Tuesday. I'll give myself the weekend to decide what to do. Perhaps I can speak to him at Brockham's on Monday, she thought. He might be the manager but it was her business and she would feel more confident there. Or I could always ring him at home rather than do it face to face. It was time to call his bluff, whatever the outcome.

Neil was the only person who could make up for the misery of her childhood. 'I was so stupid all those years ago, stupid and naïve. I can't blow it now,' she said, reaching for her book in the hope it would distract her.

The sun was hot and made her drowsy. When she woke, thirsty and with the beginning of a headache, Carmen knew what she had to do.

2

Jane Stevenson felt tired and guilty, or maybe guilty because she was tired; certainly guilty because she was sitting on a banquette in the Coach and Horses at five fifteen making a vodka and tonic last. Vodka so he would not smell it on her breath. It had been a hard day and she had shopped during her lunch hour, although she had forgotten to go into Brockham's to look for a birthday present. There never seemed to be enough hours in the day.

It had become a ritual, this calling in for a single, solitary drink on her way home from work. She needed the half-hour to herself. Not to wind down from the demands of the clients, although they were exhausting enough. They filled the rows of seats whilst they waited for their turn at the window to claim their benefits, to shout or weep or threaten in frustration at the red tape or promise to leave their children on the counter of the Social Security building. She was used to that. Jane sympathised with some, the truly desperate, and despised others.

'Swinging the lead', her father would have called it. She lit a cigarette to quell her irritation because she believed that that was what George was doing. It was the reason she had taken to calling in at the Coach and Horses instead of going straight home. It was this brief respite from both worlds that she needed, the only time now that she had to herself. George thought she finished work at five thirty. She had no intention of disillusioning him.

He had taken early retirement on the grounds of ill health. Money wasn't a problem but Jane continued to work rather than stay at home and listen to endless complaints and verbatim reports of what the doctor had said to George on one of his frequent visits to the surgery. At least the out-patients appointments were over. I wonder what happened to that nice woman and her daughter who always seemed to be there, too? Jane thought, unable for the moment to recall their names. It was some other specialist they waited to see. She sighed. Fair enough, George does have a bad back, but it isn't that bad now. And she knew his carping, his criticism of almost everything she did, was not really directed at her. It was frustration and boredom which had made him that way. He regretted retiring early and missed the camaraderie of the men with whom he had worked. His lessened mobility irked him and made him feel his age and, like many men in his position, he had no hobbies to distract him. He had been a considerate and loving husband until recently. Perhaps when their first grandchild was born in a couple of months' time the baby would provide a new interest for him.

Jane looked at her watch. In ten minutes she must leave to make her way to the underground car-park over the road then drive home and cook their evening meal, or, rather, tonight, to wash the salad. It was too hot for anything more substantial. Why couldn't George do it? She knew why. Jane had always done the cooking, he didn't know how. But it was a matter of pride that she managed to hold down a full-time job and run a household effortlessly. Or was it? Wasn't it more of a way of getting at George, of trying to show him up in the face of so much efficiency because he kept on at her? It was not an idea with which she was comfortable. It made her feel ashamed.

11

We're as bad as each other, she decided, which was sad considering the feelings they still had for one another.

These introspective thoughts made her careless as she tipped the second half of the bottle of tonic into the already diluted vodka, crushed her cigarette into the ashtray and stood up and walked towards the Ladies.

The young man serving smiled at her. She was now considered a regular. Groups of suited businessmen stood around the bar, some of them already quite loud. Couples tended to sit at the tables. Between the hours of five and seven the barman was kept busy. The Coach and Horses was situated almost opposite the new precinct which housed the Town Hall and many other municipal buildings. It had also picked up the trade from the Station Hotel after it had been pulled down to make way for a wider road.

Jane pushed open the door of the Ladies and came face to face with her own reflection. It always surprised her. In her imagination she saw herself as older, more careworn, more downtrodden. She was, in fact, smart and attractive. Having George at home had somehow sapped her strength. It's time to make a stand, to have it out with him. We can't go on like this, he's as miserable as I am, she decided as she washed her hands and dried them.

Jane returned to the table but did not sit down. She picked up her glass and swallowed the last of her drink then reached for her handbag. It wasn't there. Neither was the woman she had glimpsed briefly and would not recognise on a second occasion.

George Stevenson was watching the local news when the telephone rang. That would be Jane. She was late and he had started to worry, something was wrong. He glanced at the clock – six thirty – then lifted the receiver. Fleetingly, it crossed his mind she was phoning to say she had left him. It would be no more than he deserved. He realised what he was turning into and hated himself for it but he did not know how to alter the situation.

'Mr Stevenson?'

'Yes.' The knot in George's stomach tightened. It was an official-sounding voice.

'This is PC Gilbert. No,' he said quickly, interrupting George's question, 'no, there hasn't been an accident. Your wife's fine, just a little shaken. We're at the Coach and Horses and we're bringing her home straight away. She just wanted us to let you know she was all right.'

'Thank you.' George hung up. He was shaking. Why couldn't Jane have rung him herself? Was she that afraid of him? What was she doing in a pub, and what was wrong with the car that she needed a lift? Horrified, he wondered if Jane was drunk and had caused a scene and the landlord had called the police. Then he smiled. If so, he would have liked to witness it. Jane was always so self-controlled.

As soon as he heard a car pull up outside he went to the front door and opened it. The heat engulfed him, rising as it did from the pavement on to which the door opened. In the summer they kept the living-room blinds pulled down all day as their side of the street faced due south.

Jane was getting out of the car. George saw the the young man at the wheel and the Scandinavian-looking blonde beside him. Both were in uniform. It wouldn't have mattered if they weren't because the car had 'Police' written on both sides and a blue light on its roof, quite enough to draw a couple of their neighbours outside.

George took his wife's arm and drew her into the house. 'Are you all right?' he asked as he bent to kiss her forehead.

'Yes. I'm fine now.'

'You're as white as a sheet. I'll make you some tea.'

Jane followed him to the kitchen. It was a large room for such a small house, a house which had been built over a hundred years ago when the kitchen was not just somewhere to plug in appliances, but it was a nice room, one they both used a lot.

George filled the kettle and waited for some sort of an explanation. None was forthcoming. 'What happened, love?' He placed a mug of tea in front of her and surprised her by adding a sweetener without her having to ask.

'I went for a drink, George, that's what happened. Just the one. I do it every night. A vodka and tonic in the Coach and Horses on my way home.'

'I see.' George pulled out a chair and sat opposite her. 'I think I can understand that.'

13

'Can you?' Her voice was harder than the expression on her face. She wanted to believe him.

'Yes. And we've got some talking to do. But that can wait. Do you want to tell me what happened?'

She told him. 'And before you say it, don't bother. I already know it.' She did. And the WPC had, tactfully, pointed out her stupidity. She shook her head. Not only had she been daft enough to leave her bag on the seat, it contained everything essential: purse with the money she had drawn from the cash-point, cheque book and card, credit cards, house and car keys, driving licence, diary. But most women's handbags contained much the same, she thought. What good was a cheque book in one place, the guarantee card in another?

'Look, try not to worry about it. I'll give my mate Joe a ring and he can come and change the locks tonight. Then you get on to that number, the one where they cancel all your cards at once, there's someone there twenty-four hours a day.'

Jane laughed then. She wondered when she had last done so. 'Oh, George, I would. But the number's in my diary.'

'And the diary's in your bag.' George laughed with her.

PCs Gilbert and Saunders had reported the incident over the car radio-phone and were continuing their shift on patrol. The streets of Rickenham Green were deserted. No one stayed in town on such a beautiful evening if it could be avoided. They might get away with a quiet shift.

'What a waste of time that was. We'll never find whoever stole that bag,' Sonia Saunders commented as she admired her reflection, or as much of it as she could see, in the small mirror on the back of the turned-down visor. As the sun began its slow descent it shone straight into their faces. 'Odd though. There were plenty of possible witnesses, many of them known to each other, and nobody saw a thing.' Even for an opportunist thief it was a risky thing to do.

Pete Gilbert grunted and drove on, squinting against the sun.

Sonia was pensive. It was odd. All right, it was a stupid thing to do, leaving a handbag unattended in a pub, but the barman could not recall anyone passing Jane Stevenson's seat or leaving

14

the pub during the few minutes she was using the Ladies. But he admitted he had been serving a large round at the time. Jane Stevenson remembered seeing a woman who was no longer there when she returned from the Ladies but she had been unable to describe her. 'Still, no one's going to be daft enough to try to use the credit cards. They'll just take the cash and dump the rest.' Sonia patted her hair into place, an unnecessary gesture as the almost white strands were pulled back from her face and knotted perfectly at the nape of her neck. 'It's not as if it's a rough pub or kids use it, it's mostly business people.'

'Will you leave it? You're beginning to sound like my wife. Once she's on a subject she can't let it go.'

'I haven't met her, but your wife's one woman I do feel sorry for.'

They continued to drive around the quiet streets. Children and dogs played in the park and the few pubs which had tables outside were well patronised. If there was trouble it would not come until later, when too much alcohol combined with frayed tempers caused by the heat would act as a catalyst and the arguments and fighting would begin.

PC Sonia Saunders was thinking about her own handbag back in the locker at the station. She was a hypocrite to have lectured Jane Stevenson for having so much of importance in one place. Sonia's bag contained exactly the same items as Jane's had done.

On Friday evening, from behind his office window, Roger Pender watched the woman. She was walking purposefully and confidently down the opposite side of Saxborough Road. Her legs were bare and lightly tanned beneath a canary yellow summer dress. She had a clean, wholesome look, the sort of woman who showered and changed her underwear daily. I like the look of her, he thought, then smiled at his mental phraseology. It was true. It was more than admiration for an attractive female, less than outright lust for a nubile nymphet.

She was crossing the road, looking both ways as she stepped on to the pedestrian crossing. A careful woman. Late thirties? Roger wondered. Forty-odd, maybe, but well preserved. He put down the diet cola he was swigging from the can, wiped his hand, wet from the chilly condensation, and went to stand behind the counter of the reception area. 'It's okay, Dean. I'll see to it,' he told his salesman. The woman was walking towards him across the forecourt.

Business had been good, as it tended to be on summer weekends. Cars broke down in the heat and people had places to get to. Others, on the spur of the moment, decided to get away for a night or so. For that reason Roger stayed open until seven.

'Good evening.'

The woman smiled shyly. 'Hello. I know I've left it a bit late, but I'd like to hire a car for a couple of days.'

'Of course. Did you have anything in particular in mind? We're a bit low on choice at the moment.'

'Something small. As long as it goes, it doesn't matter. It's my weekend for visiting my mother in Saffron Walden. I go down every other one.'

'They're all regularly serviced. I can guarantee you won't have any problems.' Roger was proud of his reputation. 'Trouble with your own car?'

'You could say that. It's a long story but I won't bore you with it.'

No wedding ring, visits Mum alternate weekends, it didn't seem likely the lady was married. 'I'll show you what we've got left. The rates vary according to –'

'I know.' She looked up at him. 'I've seen your adverts in the *Rickenham Herald*.'

Money well spent then, Roger thought, especially meeting you as a bonus. 'This way.' He held the door open for her.

They were nearly blinded by the sun glinting off the hot polished metal of the rows of cars that were for sale. The ones for hire were at the side of the building.

'This one will be fine.'

Roger nodded. She had chosen a sensible two-door hatchback which didn't guzzle petrol.

Back in reception she filled out the necessary forms and produced her driving licence. Her name was Jane Stevenson. Roger noted her date of birth. He was surprised. She was forty-three. At first he had put her between thirty-seven and the age she actually was but, unusually, she looked younger close up. No wedding ring, but she had been married. There was plenty of information on a driving licence if you cared to study it. Mrs Stevenson, Jane, he had read. 'How would you like to pay?'

'Cash, if that's all right with you?'

'That's fine.'

She handed over seventy-five pounds, the inclusive cost provided the car was returned by midnight on Sunday.

'I only stay the one night.' Jane smiled. 'It's long enough. Do you stay open on Sundays?'

'Only until four, and only in the summer.'

'What about . . .?' She turned in the direction of where the car she had hired stood.

'Just park it where you can and drop the keys through the flap in the wall outside the office. It's a sort of night-safe.'

'Thanks.' She smiled again and turned to leave, the car keys in her hand.

It was almost seven. He could buy her a drink and leave Dean to lock up. She said she only stayed the one night with her mother and if she wanted the car until Sunday that presumably meant she wasn't setting off until the morning. No, better to wait until she returned. On a second meeting an invitation would not seem so pushy. He would hang around after he closed, do some paperwork until, say, six, maybe even six thirty. Longer than that would appear obvious.

Roger smiled. Not that it mattered. Her home address was in front of him, neatly printed on the insurance form she had filled in. Mrs Jane Stevenson, 17 Ardley Road, Rickenham Green. As he locked up he wondered why her face seemed vaguely familiar.

3

The breeze off the sea took the sting from the heat of the day, but carried with it minute particles of white sand. The tall grasses in the shallow dunes swayed to its rhythm. Dusk came slowly, almost imperceptibly. The brilliance of the cobalt August sky softened to lilac then darkened until summer stars, more distant than those of winter, pinpricked the royal blue dome.

One by one the house lights came on. Music and people spilled on to the terrace. Conversations took place; some in whispers where couples faced the sea, others louder, with the confidence of plentiful wine.

In front of the house the gravelled drive, the lawn and the flower-beds showed the precision of a paid gardener's hand. By the small shrubbery stood a girl. A woman who looked like a girl. Her coppery hair hung loose and shiny. Beneath the dress of gold chiffon with its silk underskirt her feet were bare. The coolness of the grass was pleasing after dancing in high heels. The strappy shoes lay on their sides. Her nails were painted bronze, in keeping with her colouring. There was a glass in her hand and tears in her eyes.

From amongst the people on the terrace a tall man appeared and walked towards her. He had slightly hunched shoulders, an ungainly walk and a badly pock-marked face. He was the kindest man on earth.

'Brenda, there you are.' He frowned and touched her arm. 'Are you crying? What is it?' He paused, afraid to hear the answer. 'You haven't had second thoughts?' His face registered the extent of his concern.

'Oh, no, Andrew. Quite the opposite.' Detective Constable Brenda Gibbons smiled. 'It's just that I'm so happy.'

Andrew Osborne exhaled with relief. Women were peculiar at times, but this was unlike Brenda, normally so down-to-earth. He was happy, too, but he didn't feel like crying. 'Come on back. They're ready to serve the food.'

She nodded and started to walk beside him. 'I still can't really believe it.'

You can't? How do you imagine I feel? he thought.

The party was a joint house-warming. They had sold their respective properties and purchased the large stone house on the coast. It was mainly Andrew's money which had financed the transaction and Brenda was still uncertain how she felt about what she considered to be a retrograde step in her fight for independence.

Hesitantly, afraid of happiness, Brenda had finally agreed to move in with Andrew. He wanted marriage, she wanted to wait. 'Let's give it a year,' Brenda had said. 'We have, to coin that

modern idiom, an awful lot of emotional baggage between us.'
Andrew had had no option other than to agree.

The move meant they had to travel into Rickenham Green
each day for work but the house and the sea compensated for the
twenty-mile round trip.

'It's a shame Ian Roper couldn't make it.'

'There's enough of a police presence as it is. In fact, almost
everyone here's connected with the law in some way or another,'
Brenda said as she glanced around at Andrew's friends – soli-
citors, barristers, clerks of the court and legal secretaries – and
her own colleagues, whom Andrew had insisted she invite –
detective constables, detective sergeants, a couple of girls from
typing and Inspector John Short who never missed out on a free
drink. Scruffy Short. At that moment he was leaning over a
curvy legal executive, one hand on the trunk of a tree as he
stared at the twin mounds of her cleavage. His brown suit,
yellow shirt and brown checked tie were clean and pressed yet
he still managed to appear unkempt. His straggling moustache
did not help. Brenda wondered why he had not brought as his
guest the woman he was rumoured to have been seeing for a
couple of years. Maybe she was married.

They had reached the house. Andrew refilled her glass, aware
that her thoughts were akin to his own. Neither of them had
much of a social life outside of work. Where were the teachers
and businessmen, the farmers and sales-people, the artisans and
tradesmen most people knew? They were both guilty of the
same defect: for too long their work had been their lives.

Brenda raised her glass. 'Here's to us. And to Mark and
Yvette.' The corners of her mouth twitched. Detective Chief
Inspector Ian Roper, renowned xenophobe, had changed his tune
when he had received some photographs of Yvette. He had
shown them all over the station with a smirk on his face, proudly
announcing that she was his son's wife-to-be. Even Ian had not
been able to resist the dark-haired, olive-skinned beauty of
Yvette.

Brockham's remained open until six on Saturdays. At five past
six Malcolm Graham watched with satisfaction as the staff com-
pleted the daily ritual of closing the store. The computerised tills

19

were turned off and covered with protective plastic hoods, stray pens were placed in drawers and the till rolls, cash and credit card slips were being collected by the heads of each department. As Sylvie Harris, deputy manager, made her rounds, checking that all was in order and that no plugs had been left switched on, the staff gathered up handbags and shopping and jackets and started to leave. 'Goodnight, Sylvie,' he said, watching her walk away erectly but self-consciously towards the now still elevator. 'Dried-up old cow,' he muttered as he made his own way out.

Down on the ground floor the security guards had locked the four sets of plate glass doors but reopened one for Malcolm.

Once bereft of customers, the piped music silenced and the sounds of humanity stilled, the atmosphere in Brockham's altered radically. It reminded Malcolm of a theatre set: the display cabinets, the stylishly dressed clay mannequins, the counters minus their uniformed staff were the props waiting only for the actors to appear.

Outside the air was humid even though the buildings were now in shadow. The High Street was quiet: the shoppers had all gone now and it was too early for revellers. St Luke's church clock struck the quarter-hour. He would be home by half-past six. The evening lay ahead of him.

He got into his car and started the engine. 'That's my world,' he said as he drove past the impressive frontage of Brockham's. 'My little domain.' He grinned, showing his pointed incisors. 'Well, one of them, anyway.' Another was his life in the village, the third, well, that was something else again.

He overtook Sylvie, who walked to work, and tooted the horn. She did not respond. Women, he thought. She shouldn't have asked for it. Perhaps it was the heatwave but even Carmen was behaving oddly. It was as if she wanted to say something to him but did not know how to go about it, or could not bring herself to begin.

Elaine Pritchard was another one. He'd done her a favour by moving her from Lighting to Cosmetics. She'd thanked him politely and got on with the job but he'd expected a bit more gratitude. Yes, she had adapted to her new role quickly and with very little training, and she related well to people, but it was Malcolm who had anticipated that she would and this was one of the ways in which he had made himself indispensable.

20

He left the suburbs of Rickenham Green and drove along country roads until he reached Frampton. He pulled into his tarmacked driveway, still smiling, the lines between nostrils and mouth deeper. Tomorrow, Sunday, was his favourite day, the only day upon which he now indulged himself, when he perused the contents of the spare room cupboard. He had taken a chance with Caroline Innes, he would not make that mistake again. For almost a month he had sweated, wondering if she would say anything. He had underestimated her spirit. But that was some time ago.

The detached garage was to the left of the house and slightly back from it. He drove into it, locked the door behind him then walked towards the house. In front of the garage was a small shrubbery, then the drive. To its right was an emerald lawn, the vertical stripes a pleasure to look at, especially on a hot August evening. It was edged with floribunda roses which disguised the low brick wall behind them. Malcolm nodded. The garden, like most of his life, was under perfect control. 'You're too damn fussy,' his mother used to complain, which was odd when she had expected so much of him.

In the cheerful red and yellow kitchen he made tea and took it outside where he could enjoy further proof of his diligence. Before him spread another lawn, much larger than at the front. Against the high lattice-work fences which surrounded the back of the property, clematis, honeysuckle and cotoneaster had been espaliered. In the borders beneath grew delphiniums and hollyhocks, foxgloves and tiger-lilies, and in front of them flourished lower, ground-cover plants: staggered tiers of varying colours which blended and were pleasing to the eye. The two apple trees bore fruit, not yet quite ready to pick, and the small vegetable patch produced runner-beans and strawberries, and sprouts and cabbage in the winter.

The tea was hot. Steam rose in a straight line from the teacup which rested on its saucer on the varnished wooden garden table. Soon he would prepare his solitary meal but first he would bath and change out of his lightweight business suit into casual trousers and a polo shirt. The rotary line next door creaked as Amy Talbot took in her washing. Why don't they oil the bloody thing? Malcolm wondered. It had been creaking for years. He swatted a wasp as it hovered over the scented China tea.

The sun was still hot on his head. Heat had built up over the course of the day and had warmed the crazy-paving of the patio and the wood of the bench upon which he sat. The scent of the potted geraniums filled the air and there was a summer stillness which was relaxing. He got up and went inside to have a bath.

'No one would guess you were sixty,' he told his naked reflection as he towelled himself dry. He studied his firm, lean body from both sides then ran a hand through his silvery hair. It might be almost white, but there's plenty of it, he thought with pride rather than vanity.

The sun began to slide imperceptibly towards the horizon. Shadows lengthened fractionally as Malcolm collected his tea things from the garden. He rinsed them under the tap and left them by the sink to drain. He took the pot and emptied the leaves around the thorny stem of a rose bush then went inside to prepare his meal.

He had got no further than pouring a large glass of chilled white Australian when the telephone rang. He glanced at his watch. Five past seven. It was too early to be John or Amy Talbot, who sometimes invited him to join their drinks or card parties at the weekend. He rarely accepted now because it was always the same crowd and he had tired of their conversation. But they were decent people and pleasant enough to have as neighbours.

'Hello?' Malcolm frowned, not recognising the voice at first because it did not belong to anyone who had rung him at home before. He listened, feeling a little sick. This might mean a police investigation. 'I see. Are you sure? Then of course you must come. Yes, as soon as you can get here.'

He replaced the receiver, trembling a little, glad he had not already poured his second glass of wine because he needed it now. Two large glasses were normally his limit. But the idea that Sylvie Harris was fiddling the store was unbelievable, at odds with her character even if she was a cold bitch. However, it seemed there was proof. It would need to be checked before he came to a decision. He could not go running to the police with a false allegation against a member of his staff, his deputy at that, and come out of it looking good. Maybe that was what was

22

bothering Carmen, maybe she already knew and wondered why he had done nothing about it.

He checked his watch again. His guest would be arriving soon. He refilled his glass and took it out to the garden where he paced up and down. The air was warm and balmy. At the bottom of the garden a swarm of midges hovered between the shrubs. 'Hurry up,' he muttered. 'I want to get this over with.'

The Talbots, too, were outside, he could hear their voices as they shared the task of watering the plants.

He continued to pace, for once unable to enjoy his garden. Then he smiled. Once the business part of the evening was out of the way there might be a chance he could turn the rest of it to his advantage.

'Hello.'

The quiet voice took him by surprise. He spun around. His visitor had come around the side of the house. It was not the one he had been expecting.

4

It had rained in Reims. To lessen the length of the journey they had shunned the ferry and flown to Paris where they'd hired a car at Charles de Gaulle airport. Ian hated flying and he wasn't very keen on rain. They were now on their way home. It seemed impossible so much had occurred in such a short time.

But everything had happened so fast. Or maybe he had not been taking it in. When Mark had come home from Italy for Christmas he had mentioned a French girlfriend, a fellow artist he had met in Castellammare where they both lived and worked. All Ian knew about the place was that it was on the coast and not far from Naples. Yvette's name came up more frequently in Mark's letters and weekly telephone calls but there had been other girls before. Many times Moira had hinted that this was different, this was serious, trying to soften him up, Ian guessed. And now his son had married her. A French girl who was now his daughter-in-law. They had only met her on Friday, along with her family, but she was as lovely as she appeared in the photographs. And her English was perfect. A definite plus point. Along with Moira's mother, Philippa, they had dined late in a restaurant as guests of Hervé Dupois. Ian discovered Yvette's parents were on an equal footing. They hardly knew Mark and were as bemused as himself. They, too, spoke excellent English and Moira did not show him up by talking to them in French all the time.

'Yes, all right,' he admitted as they waited to board their flight back, 'they're charming.'

'And rich.'

'I know.' From what he had learned of the Dupois family, Moira could not be accused of hyperbole. They were stinking rich.

'And Mum liked them.'

Ian glanced at his mother-in-law who was browsing in the airport gift shop. 'Your mother can't see bad in anyone.' He caught Moira's expression and held out his hands. 'Not that I'm suggesting there is anything bad to see.'

'She liked *you* right from the start.'

'Well, there. See what I mean?' Ian grinned, catching sight of himself in a plate glass window. He'd begun to worry about the grey appearing at his temples but Hervé Dupois, Yvette's father, was completely grey and extremely distinguished. Perhaps it didn't matter after all.

Philippa Lawrence had fitted in with her soon-to-be in-laws immediately. Widowed many years previously, she had not allowed herself to grow old or bitter, and she had kept her looks. Her gold hair had faded a little and was now worn up, looping softly above her ears and pinned in a neat roll. She was the perfect example of the old adage about looking at the mother before marrying the daughter. Ian knew he was a lucky man; a delightful mother-in-law, a lovely wife who still caught men's eyes and now a beautiful daughter-in-law had joined the family.

Their flight left on time. Moira sat next to Philippa, who closed her eyes as soon as they were airborne. The journey and the excitement had tired her. Moira leant back in her seat and relived the wedding.

After a tour of the cathedral she and Ian had returned to the hotel with its heavy dark furniture and shuttered windows and wrestled with the antiquated plumbing. 'It makes ours seem positively sophisticated,' Ian had grumbled before discovering that the shower, once mastered, was hot and efficient. 'You're shaking,' he'd said later as Moira got ready. Slender and blonde, she only reached his chin. Mostly he managed to forget the fifteen years separating them, but at least he didn't look bad for his age.

'I know. I knew it would probably happen at some time, but seeing your only child married is hopefully a once in a lifetime event. Imagine how Yvette must be feeling. And Mark.' Once my baby, my only child, she had added silently.

At three fifty they were shown to their seats at the front of the church. Ian, Moira and Philippa, Mark's only relations. Behind them were young faces, Mark's friends, some of whom they knew. To Moira's left was Mark, his hands clasped in front of his thighs as he peered down the aisle anxiously. She could not meet his eye in case she started crying. He's a man now, she remembered thinking, and about to become a husband.

When the subdued organ music swelled and every head turned she had swallowed hard. Yvette, in a dress and veil she would remember all her life, walked slowly towards them alongside her father. Moira had felt the first prickle of tears.

When Mark made his responses Moira had pressed her lips together tightly, but it was no good. The lump in her throat grew bigger and she had had to find a tissue to wipe her eyes. Across the aisle Solange Dupois, the bride's mother, was crying openly.

Once the religious ceremony was over the atmosphere had changed. Photographs were taken amidst laughter before everyone followed the bride and groom the short distance to the offices where the brief civil ceremony took place. Hired cars took them back to the hotel where the reception was being held.

'It was a beautiful wedding,' Philippa commented once the dancing had begun.

'You didn't cry. It's traditional at weddings,' Moira had admonished.

'No. I can't see the point in wasting tears on happiness.'

'Will they be happy, do you think?'

'I don't know, darling, any more than I did when you married Ian.'

'But you said you liked him, that you thought he was just right for me.'

'I did, and do like him, but what I thought was right for you didn't make it necessarily true. Anyway, you've stuck together this long so I can't have been far out. Ah, a slow tune. Go and get him to dance with you. Look at him skulking in that corner.'

'Dance? Ian?'

Philippa had laughed. 'Yes. Sorry, I forgot.' She had never met a man less able to follow a beat and it was rarely that he could be persuaded on to the dance floor.

Mark and Yvette were going to Singapore – the trip was a wedding present from her parents. 'I'm glad we had a son,' Ian had said when he had estimated the cost of the wedding and honeymoon. Their own gifts had been chosen from a list Yvette had provided. Ian had added a generous cheque.

They landed mid-afternoon. Ironically, heat shimmered over the runway and the trip seemed to be in reverse. It had rained the whole time they were in France. Landing at Heathrow was more akin to stepping off a plane in the Mediterranean than coming home. At least the car, in the depths of the long-stay car-park, was cool.

They were mostly silent on the drive home, each of them thinking about Mark and his future. It wasn't true that you gained a daughter, Moira realised. Her son was married. He would always be her son, of course, but he now belonged to another woman. She felt like crying again. Glancing over her shoulder, she saw that Philippa looked pale. She tended to forget her mother was no longer a young woman.

'I'm just tired, darling,' Philippa said, interpreting the worried look. 'I'll be fine after a good night's sleep.'

'I wonder how the Ugly Brute's party went?' Ian said after they'd dropped Philippa off and had left the A12 and were heading towards Rickenham Green. Now he was back on home territory he felt more normal, more like himself. 'I don't know what that girl sees in him.'

'I do wish you wouldn't call him that. He's not ugly. And you'll let it slip out in front of him one day if you're not careful.'

'I've never been able to understand what women find attractive. At least you're lucky, you've got me.'

'I was thinking of buying you a drink in the Crown once we'd unpacked. But I've just decided you can pay.'

'Suits me. I'm gasping for an English pint.'

Moira smiled. He had grumbled enough about the lack of real ale on the Continent, although she had noticed it had not stopped him drinking any of the wines which were offered. And she knew how it would be in the pub. Bob Jones and his wife Connie would naturally ask how things had gone. Ian, who had enjoyed himself far more than he would ever admit, would render a detailed account. And they say women gossip, Moira thought. But she had to hand it to Ian, not once had he made a disparaging remark about foreigners. In fact, she realised as they turned into the familiar vista of Belmont Terrace, he was rather impressed by the Dupois family. As I was, she thought. And at least the young artists have somewhere to turn if they don't succeed.

5

Detective Chief Inspector Ian Roper felt he had been away from home for far longer than forty-eight hours. The journey to Reims and back seemed to have taken it out of him. He refused to consider there might be an emotional element. He slept fitfully on Sunday night, too hot beneath the duvet, not warm enough on top of it, conscious that he needed sleep because work awaited him in the morning. Beside him, Moira seemed unconcerned by the heat. She lay on her side serenely, one arm folded across her chest on top of the covers.

Daylight came early. Ian switched off the clock-radio alarm before it blared into life, an unusual action as he was capable of sleeping through it if the snooze button had not been activated. He shaved and showered in lukewarm water then made a pot of tea, taking some up to Moira.

'Is something wrong?' She sat up and took the mug from Ian's extended hand. He envied her her ability to open her eyes and be instantly alert.

'No. I was hot, I didn't sleep well.'

'They'll be there now, Singapore. It can be very humid, I believe. Is it their summertime?'

'Moira, I've absolutely no idea. I'm sure they'll enjoy themselves whatever the weather.'

'Don't snap, it's not my fault you're tired.'

'I'm sorry. It's just that I didn't expect to feel so, well, so different when Mark got married. Older, I mean.'

Moira sighed. There was hardly a day when someone or something did not remind him of his own mortality. It was odd in such a strong, healthy man. 'God only knows what you'll be like when you're a grandfather,' she said more sharply than she had intended as she swung her slender legs over the side of the bed.

His mouth dropped open. 'She's not –'

'No, Ian. Not as far as I'm aware,' Moira interrupted.

They ate toast in the garden. It was already hot and, according to the weather forecast which they could hear on the radio through the open kitchen window, there was more of the same to come.

By eight thirty Detective Chief Inspector Roper had already been updated as to the events of the weekend. They corresponded almost exactly with those of the previous one: the usual spate of petty crimes.

Just as he finished reading what he thought was relevant DC Brenda Gibbons appeared in the doorway of the general office. He remembered she had now moved in with her boyfriend, Andrew Osborne, and the party he had missed because of the wedding. His social life was all or nothing. He felt avuncular, ready to offer advice to the female half of this latest coupling from what he now considered to be his experience of youthful liaisons. Except Brenda was almost thirty and had one violent marriage behind her. 'How was the party?' he asked with a smile.

'It was lovely.' Brenda dropped her shoulder-bag on to the seat behind her desk. Her coppery hair shone in the shafts of sunlight flowing through the gaps between the slats of the blinds. Someone had been thoughtful enough to lower them along the length of the windowed wall. 'And how was the wedding?'

'It couldn't have gone better. I'll bring the photographs in when we get them back.'

Brenda raised a curved eyebrow and grinned at Inspector Short who had entered the room, only ten minutes late, as Ian replied. It was unlike the Chief to bring his personal life to work.

'Morning.' Beads of sweat stood out on John Short's forehead. The strands of hair which failed to conceal his baldness were plastered to his scalp. His light grey trousers had a neat crease but there was a mark on his shirt and his shoes were scuffed. It was one of his better days. He sat down and placed a full container of machine coffee perilously close to the keyboard of his computer terminal. 'Great party, Brenda. Osborne's obviously got a bob or two. No wonder you decided to move in with him, this job pays bugger all.'

'Did you score with the legal exec?' she retaliated, having seen the well-endowed woman duck out from under his arm and make a quick get-away.

'Nope. But you can't win them all.' Scruffy Short tugged at his moustache in a manner which suggested he might find something useful amongst the pepper and salt strands.

Ian was on his third cup of coffee by the time the pile of paperwork on his desk finally appeared to be diminishing. He sat back in his chair, his hands clasped behind his head, and stretched. It was too hot to work even though the window behind him was wide open. Traffic sounds drifted up along with the occasional high-pitched voice of a child.

Ian rocked forwards allowing the front legs of his chair to regain contact with the floor when DC Alan Campbell tapped politely on the open door.

'Sir, we've got a suspicious death. Inspector Short and DC Gibbons are on their way to Frampton now.'

'Oh?' Ian met Alan's light blue eyes. His face was paler than ever beneath the sandy hair.

'It's a murder actually.'

Ian frowned. Campbell was a pedant. Nothing was given a name or taken for granted until it could be proved. 'Any details?'

'Not many. But from the way the response officers described the scene there can't be any doubt.'

'The address?' Ian was already on his feet as Alan recited it. He pulled the knot of his tie closer to his neck. However hot it was he never turned up for work without one. Then he followed Alan Campbell down the stairs. Knowing that Inspector Short would be in charge of the case did not prevent him from attending the scene. It was the way in which he liked to work.

A car was waiting. They were driven through the baking heat of the town centre. It could almost have been a Sunday, the streets were so quiet. There were very few shoppers. It was eleven forty, too soon for office and shop workers to be eating their sandwiches in the park or on the seats in the modern precinct where the municipal buildings stood, a little way up from the police station. There were a few trees and a fountain in the centre which gave an illusion of coolness.

As soon as they left Rickenham Green the scenery became rural. It was a town which ended abruptly on all sides. There was now a bypass to the east but there were no straggling suburbs. Rows of houses were replaced immediately with narrow roads which wound beneath the overhanging branches of trees, now in full leaf. The hedgerows were overgrown with an abundance of wild flowers. Small brown butterflies rose then settled again after the car had passed by. They turned into a wider road where the view was more typical of Suffolk. The countryside was flat and could be seen far into the distance until the land and the horizon became a blur in the heat haze.

A small sign at the side of the road welcomed them to Frampton and asked them to drive carefully through the village. Sensible advice, Ian thought, but it suggested that once you had passed through you had permission to tear through the lanes at ninety miles an hour.

There were no houses until a couple of hundred yards after the sign. The first few they passed were large, detached properties. They stood deserted, silent and somnolent in the midday heat. Next came the village: a straggle of small cottages and a few shops, one of which had gone the way of other village shops, those that had survived. It had turned into a mini-supermarket; to Ian the oxymoron was more baffling than most. There were two pubs, one catering to the locals, the other frequented by tourists and men who wanted somewhere more comfortable to take their wives.

Inured to squeamishness after so many years in the job, Ian still hated the sight of death, especially when it was premature.

Beside him, Alan Campbell, never garrulous, was more silent than usual. Ian suspected he had some idea of what to expect.

They drew up in a quiet lane which ran at right angles to the main street of the village of Frampton. There was no one around. Half a dozen detached houses lined one side. They were small but solidly built and varied only a little in their owners' choice of paintwork and the layout of the front gardens. The body of the victim lay in number three.

A uniformed officer stood at the top of the small drive outside the front door. He had his notebook in his hand and was responsible for recording the movements of those coming and going which, so far, consisted only of himself and his colleagues, DC Gibbons and Inspector Short. Now there were two more names to add, DC Campbell's and the Chief Inspector's. PC Henderson was well aware that the Chief need not have put in an appearance, but he was also aware that DCI Roper liked to be in on everything from the start.

Ian nodded at the uniformed officer. His colleague sat in the passenger seat of the patrol car with the door flung open. He looked ill.

Ian reached the front door, Alan Campbell a few paces behind him. Before anyone had a chance to speak, Brenda Gibbons flew down the stairs, staggered along the hallway and, unable to help herself, left her own fingerprints on the door frame as she steadied herself. She glanced at Ian, white-faced and wide-eyed, shook her head then lurched a couple of steps to one side where she vomited into a flower-bed.

Ian, allowing her time to recover, turned his back. 'What's the story?'

PC Henderson introduced himself before explaining the situation. He recognised the Chief but was unsure whether the reverse applied. 'A woman from Brockham's named Sylvia Harris rang in when the store manager didn't turn up for work. He's been with them for twenty-one years and has never been late. Punctuality's a bit of an obsession with him, apparently, and he's always there six days a week. She said he's had the occasional day off for illness or a few hours for the dentist but that's all, and he's always let them know before. She telephoned him here but there was no answer.'

'What's his name?'

31

'Malcolm Graham.'

Ian could imagine the type: neat, fussy and punctilious. His immaculate garden hinted at this. And for a fellow employee to call the police after only a couple of hours meant his absence was very unusual. 'Go on.'

'Mrs Harris said she rang again an hour later but got no joy. He lives on his own, that's as much as she could tell us, and she thought he might've had a heart attack or something equally serious if he couldn't get to the phone. Her father had a heart attack at the same age, sixtyish, so she was worried.'

'And you were asked to take a look.'

PC Henderson nodded then swallowed hard. His face had a greenish tinge. Ian suddenly did not want to enter that house. 'We knocked but couldn't get any reply. There's a car in the garage. It's locked but you can see it through the side window. And the bedroom curtains were closed. We broke in through the back door.'

Entry and search without warrant, but it was all right. Section 17 of the 1984 PACE Act allowed this for the purpose of saving life or limb. However, in this case they had been too late – how late they may or may not find out. Even an estimated time of death allowing several hours either side could be way off the mark. Ian pictured Henderson and his colleague poking around, sizing up the situation and believing Mrs Harris's theory to be correct: Malcolm Graham, if that was the name of the person inside the house, had been taken ill, had possibly died in his sleep. Obviously he had not.

Only minutes had passed since his arrival but Ian could postpone the moment no longer. He had to go inside. 'Are you all right, Brenda?'

She was wiping her mouth with a tissue, pale beneath her suntan, sweat standing out on her high brow. She smoothed down the skirt of her blue and white summer dress and raised her head. 'Yes, sir. I'm fine now, thanks.' It was the first time Ian had seen her look anything other than calm, cool and in control.

The hall was carpeted in expensive-looking pea-green wool but it was too narrow to hold any furniture. A couple of small charcoal sketches hung on the walls. The door to the sitting-room stood open showing tasteful furnishing and decoration.

But Malcolm Graham probably got a good discount at Brockham's. Behind this was another, smaller room. Ian ignored it as he did the downstairs toilet and kitchen because PC Henderson was indicating that the body lay upstairs.

The boards creaked as they took Ian's weight but he was careful not to touch the wooden banister. John Short appeared from a bedroom, holding a mobile phone into which he was speaking. Ian waited until he had finished summoning the team of people requisite at the scene of a crime. He looked unflustered, maybe it wasn't as bad as he'd feared. But it was, Ian knew that. There was blood, a lot of it, he could smell it in the hall. And it wasn't fresh.

The bedroom door was open, but not fully, and it was dim inside the room. The curtains must have been lined to keep out the brilliant sunshine. Ian saw only the corner of the bed and an inch or so of the striped duvet cover. He braced himself. Along with the unmistakable smell of blood was the added smell of death, of the onset of putrefaction.

Short met his eyes but said nothing as he elbowed the door until it was fully open.

'Oh, Christ!' Ian took an involuntary step backwards. His chest was tight as he struggled for breath. Bile rose in his throat, he swallowed it, then a second time. For several seconds he could not believe what he was seeing, he could not think let alone speak. 'What in God's name have we got here?' he finally croaked. He closed his eyes but when he opened them nothing in that room had altered.

A man, what had once been a man, lay spread-eagled on the bed. He was naked. Around him the bedclothes were saturated with blood, darker at the edges of the stains where it had started to dry first. There were several stab wounds to his chest. They were nothing. Between his legs, where his penis had once been, the flesh was mangled and the blood had pooled. The penis itself lay next to his knee. His eyes were open but whether the surprise in them was real or imagined, Ian was unsure. The latter, he supposed, as the pupils had already clouded over. It would not require an expert to establish cause of death.

They waited outside, in various states of shock or horror, until the members of the team began to arrive. No one spoke. The tableau inside that house was incomprehensible. It was also incongruous against the beauty of the surrounding countryside bathed in the drowsy heat of a perfect summer's day. Bees nestled in the heart of each flower before moving on to the next one; in the distance a dog barked twice, the sound carrying in the still air and momentarily shattering the silence.

Ian studied the neatness of everything, the weeded flower-beds, the striped lawn and the carefully tended tubs. Illogically, he found there was something more oddly disturbing in the perennials drooping in the heat than in what lay on the bed. They might have been dying too, and would do so now there was no one to water them.

The sound of an engine changing gear brought them back to life, as if they had been actors waiting for a cue. Within minutes there seemed to be more people present than the house could accommodate, but each of them knew the routine and began to get on with it.

'The incident room, sir, where will it be?' Alan Campbell asked, knowing they were too far from Rickenham Green to use what they referred to there as the murder room.

'I'm not sure. The village hall, if it's not in use.' There was one, purpose-built not many years previously and therefore a more substantial structure than some even if it was ugly.

There was little Ian could do now other than wait. 'Thorne knows?' he asked Short.

'Yes.'

Ian nodded. Superintendent Thorne was due to go on leave. He would want this cleared up before he did so. Not that he would make impossible demands, he was a fair man and well liked and did not mind that his West Midlands accent was a cause of amusement and imitation, much of it inaccurate.

Later, when the pathologist had been and gone, when the body had been removed to the mortuary and the SOCOs had finished their assiduous tasks, the rest of the house would receive attention. Somewhere inside, some small, seemingly unimportant thing might lead them to a motive, might even lead them to the killer. Impatient as he was to start, Ian knew he would have to wait.

When the Home Office pathologist finally arrived he took one look at the officers assembled in the front garden and knew that here was something different. He spoke briefly to Ian then, his bag in his hand, made his way upstairs. Meticulously, and without speaking, he examined the body, disturbing as little as possible. He refused to be more specific regarding the time of death other than to suggest it had probably occurred within the last thirty-six hours. 'Rigor's almost worn off,' he added with a shrug.

Ian knew what he meant. The stiffening usually began within a couple of hours. It would last about a day and take approximately the same amount of time to wear off, but in a heatwave like this the process would have been speeded up. But what the pathologist didn't know, and he did, was that Sylvie Harris had seen Malcolm Graham alive and well at a quarter past six on Saturday night when he drove past her on his way home. And he might have been seen since that time by any of his neighbours. Ian groaned. 'Never make assumptions' was one of his favourite phrases. He had just done so. They did not know that the man on the bed was Malcolm Graham.

A car turned into the lane and slowed outside the gate, not from curiosity but in order to negotiate the gate next door. Whoever was driving could not have failed to see the activity at number three. It was too good an opportunity to miss. Chief Inspector Roper sent Brenda and Alan around to question the neighbour.

By six o'clock the village hall was on its way to becoming an incident room although some of the electronic equipment had not arrived and the telephone wasn't working. Officers were engaged to man the hall, including DC Campbell who excelled at collating information and for whom computers might have been invented.

Ian and John Short returned to Rickenham, already loaded down with boxes which contained what might turn out to be evidence. As yet they had no official identification of the body, although the likelihood was that it was that of Malcolm Graham. They knew nothing about him so far, other than that he had worked at Brockham's for twenty-one years.

'It's me, love,' Ian said when Moira answered the phone. 'Something's come up, but I'll try and get back as early as I can.'

'That's all right. I'm going out for a drink with the people from work. I did tell you.'

Yes, you probably did, Ian thought. Why can I never remember things like that? 'See you later.' He hung up. He could have delegated the mundane task but to deflect the images of that mutilated body which kept pushing their way to the front of his mind he began to sift through the papers in the box in front of him.

6

Coffee breaks were over and although the early lunches had begun the staff room usually remained empty at midday. No one brought sandwiches and flasks any longer. They were time-consuming to prepare and barely economical because the restaurant meals were subsidised for employees and the ambience there was far more convivial. Sylvia Harris, who was known to everyone as Sylvie, needed a few minutes alone. She sat in a floral-patterned armchair directly beneath a 'No Smoking' sign and lit up. She crossed her long, thin legs and examined her scarlet nails. Even in the height of summer her suits and shoes were black, clothes chosen to accentuate what she thought of as her trim figure but which only emphasised her scrawniness.

She inhaled deeply, wondering what the police would think of her for telephoning so quickly. But they did not know Malcolm. For him not to turn up, not to telephone, something had to be seriously wrong. It was pointless to worry, the staff would back her up, there were few who had not commented upon his absence because they could not recall a day when he had not been there. Some were genuinely concerned, others merely curious.

Sylvie knew her excitement must not be allowed to show. She also felt vaguely sick, ashamed of what she was thinking. If something had happened to him, Malcolm's job would become hers – Carmen Brockham had more or less said so in the eventuality of his retirement. As head of the store she would earn the respect due to her, and she would not have to suffer that awful feeling of Malcolm's eyes burning into her back.

It isn't fair, I've played second fiddle for far too long, she thought as she stubbed out the cigarette in a saucer. But there was no time to ponder the injustices of life because her bleeper went off. Her presence was required in the footwear department where a disgruntled customer was trying to return a pair of shoes as unsuitable when they had obviously had a lot of wear.

'No news yet?' This refrain was echoed in each department as Sylvie passed through them in her temporary capacity as store manager. With the extra responsibility she had not noticed how late it was. The working day was almost over and the police had not been back to her. 'No. No news,' she replied. Ought she to ring again, or would it be better to contact Carmen? Of course, it would be Carmen to whom they would impart any relevant information, not herself. It hadn't crossed her mind to ring her herself. Why Carmen had kept Malcolm on was a mystery. He didn't actually do anything. 'Anyway, I expect we'll find out soon enough,' she added with a tight smile to each inquiry.

At five forty she picked up her black leather handbag and made her way home.

Although she had a car she walked to and from work as a way of keeping fit. Her house was on the Bradley estate, which comprised three cul-de-sacs of houses built in the seventies. She had remained there after her divorce, the property paid for by her husband in return for his freedom. She had no desire to move, the house suited her and she got on with her neighbours. But now, if she had Malcolm's job, she could afford the minor alterations she wanted and she could buy some new furniture.

Malcolm had been to the house only once. Sylvie, mistakenly, had imagined a different scenario from the one which had taken place.

The coolness of the house, which was shaded by tall trees at the back, was welcome after the walk home. Sylvie drank a glass of water then opened the kitchen door. The small back garden was in shadow. She would sit out there with a cup of tea and relax. There wouldn't be many more such nights so late in the year.

A quiet evening, that's what I need, she decided as she drank her tea and surveyed the patchy lawn. She wasn't much of a gardener. I won't even think about Malcolm. I've done the right thing, if the police haven't acted upon the information I gave them it's hardly my fault.

37

Later, when she was just settling down to watch a film, Carmen rang with the news that Malcolm was dead. There was no way of forgetting him that night.

DC Brenda Gibbons felt ashamed. She had fought the waves of nausea but they had overcome her. When her mouth filled with bile for a third time she had had to get out of the house before she contaminated the scene but even then she had managed to leave her fingerprints on the doorframe. No one had chastised her and she had felt a little better knowing that the pale-faced PC sitting in the patrol car had also been sick.

When the Chief sent them to question the neighbour she was ready for it, welcomed it, in fact, if it meant avoiding that bedroom.

She and Alan walked up the drive of number four Spring Lane. The sun beat down on their heads, merciless in the mid-afternoon. Heat shimmered over the sticky tarmac and the air was heady with the scent of roses. A car stood to one side, its boot open. Before they reached the front door an elderly but sprightly man appeared from around the side of the house. The exposed parts of his body were deeply tanned in the way only possible for someone who was able to take advantage of every hour of sunshine. His small moustache was clipped neatly but his eyebrows had not received the same treatment. They gave him a slightly startled expression.

'Good afternoon. Can I help you?' His voice was low and polite but accentless.

It was Brenda who introduced them, taking the lead as she always did although she and Alan were of equal rank.

'Ah, yes. I couldn't help but notice the cars next door. I'm John Talbot. Has something happened to Malcolm?'

'We think so. There has been an incident at number three.' Brenda hated herself for the jargon and avoided Alan's eyes. She could hardly say that the man's neighbour lay dead, stark naked and dismembered. Her stomach heaved. She closed her eyes and breathed deeply until the picture went away. And what was Alan thinking? Alan, whose wife, ex-wife for some time now, had been taking part in hard core pornography, a fact he had witnessed for himself during the course of an investigation. Bad enough for anyone, but for the puritanical Scotsman it must have been devastating. When he had stepped into the bedroom next door his expression had held more disgust than shock or pity. Something so obviously sexual, so filled with hate, must have brought back unwelcome memories.

'Won't you come in, please? My wife's in the kitchen. I'll just get the last couple of bags. We always shop on Mondays to avoid the crowds.'

They followed the direction in which he had gestured with a hand. The path led around the side of the house to the back door. Brenda nodded in satisfaction. Ahead lay her sort of garden, cared for but not regimented like the one to their right. The effect here was more subtle and therefore more soothing.

'Hello.' Mrs Talbot looked up in surprise. She was holding several wrapped packets of cold meat from a supermarket delicatessen counter prior to stacking them in the fridge.

'It's the police, dear. This is my wife, Amy,' her husband said as he approached and placed two plastic carrier bags on the worktop.

'I'll make tea.' Amy Talbot spoke so decisively, as if she knew that this was the correct protocol when police officers visited, that no one demurred.

'Shall we go through to the lounge?' John Talbot stood awkwardly behind a chair. He was far less confident than his wife.

'We're fine here, if that suits you.' Brenda saw that this couple had certain standards and that entertaining in the kitchen was not one of them, but as it was less formal they might be more inclined to talk about Malcolm Graham.

'Mr Talbot, can you tell us when you last saw your neighbour?' Alan asked, knowing it was time he said something. He and Brenda had pulled out chairs. Talbot joined them, his hands clasped loosely on the table.

'Is he dead?' he asked. It was hardly a surprising question, not in view of the amount of cars and vans parked outside the house next door.

'I'm afraid I can't answer that at the moment.' They weren't yet certain that the dead man was Malcolm Graham.

Talbot nodded. 'I see. Saturday. He came home from work as

usual on Saturday evening. We heard the car. That was around six thirty.'

'You saw him?'

'No. Not then. We heard him put the car away but we didn't actually see him until later. What time did we go outside, Amy?'

'About seven.' She brought the tea things to the table and placed the pot on a ceramic tile then sat down herself.

'That's right. I remember now. We were watering the garden when I saw Malcolm walking up and down with a glass in his hand. I don't know why, but I got the impression he was waiting for someone.' He paused. 'I think because he doesn't usually display signs of restlessness. I've seen him weeding, an hour or more at a time on one bed, or reading, just relaxed in a chair. He's not one of those people who has to keep on the move. Yes, I'm sure that's why I noticed him. You can see through the hedge in several places.' Talbot dropped his eyes, sure that his guests thought he had been spying.

'You're certain it was him?'

'No question about it. He was wearing a lime green polo shirt. He's such a conservative dresser for work but at weekends he goes for – what do they call them? Hot colours.' It was said with a hint of disapproval; both he and his wife were dressed in shades of cream and beige. 'And his hair, of course. It's unmistakable. Still so very thick and white.'

Alan glanced at Brenda. This was almost as good as an identification. The polo shirt hanging over the back of the chair was the shade described by Talbot, as were the colour and texture of the dead man's hair.

'He occasionally joins us when we have people over,' Amy Talbot said, studying her plump freckled hands which lay, palms down, on her knees. 'But not so much recently.' The police were being cagey but there would not be so many of their vehicles unless something dreadful had happened to Malcolm and she felt a need to explain herself. 'He came here often when he first he moved in, but after that he frequently made an excuse even though we knew he didn't go out.'

'Was there a disagreement?' Brenda asked.

'Oh, no, nothing like that. He was always pleasant when our

paths did cross, but with him out at work all day and us visiting our family at the weekends it wasn't that often.'

Another hour passed but they learned little of any use. Malcolm Graham enjoyed his garden; he was a polite, quiet neighbour who rarely entertained although he did go out several nights each week. 'He belongs to the Elms and goes there on Wednesdays,' Talbot added. 'I recall him mentioning that, and the theatre, and he usually put in an appearance at local events, the fête, you know, that sort of thing. Most people here know him to speak to but he's not a man you can get close to.'

The Talbots had not seen Malcolm on Sunday because they had set off early to visit their grandchildren. It was still daylight when they returned so no lights would have been burning to indicate whether or not Malcolm Graham was at home. He slept at the back of the house, the windows overlooking the garden, so the drawn curtains would also have escaped their notice.

'One last question,' Alan said as he stood up to leave. 'Can you recall what time Mr Graham went back inside the house after you saw him walking around the garden?'

'No. I'm sorry. We went in ourselves about ten minutes later. We were expecting people so I didn't think any more about it.' Talbot shook his head. 'After that I don't recall hearing or seeing anything. And we would have done – if there'd been a car, I mean. We were playing bridge in the lounge with the windows open.'

'We'll need the names of your guests. It's just possible one of them may have noticed something.'

It was Amy Talbot who got up and copied them down from the small address book she kept in her handbag. There were three couples, all of whom lived within a two-mile radius.

'Eighteen years,' Brenda said as they went next door to collect the car. 'It's a long time to live in a small village. Someone must know something about him.'

They drove back to headquarters in silence, each thinking of their own past and realising that no matter what they had suffered, it was nothing compared with what had befallen the man whose murder they were investigating.

'He's got a wife. Or had one.' John Short had removed his tan linen jacket. The armpits of his brown shirt were ringed with sweat and his paunch disguised the fact that he was wearing a belt to hold up his trousers. In his hand was a marriage certificate. 'They tied the knot in June 1964, here in Rickenham at St Luke's. Someone called Diane Hicks.'

'So where is she now?' Ian asked rhetorically. 'The Harris woman who rang us said he lived alone, and the Talbots confirmed it.'

The forensic team were still at the house and would remain there for some hours to come. Inspector Short and DC Gibbons had returned with their scant information and were about to speak to Carmen Brockham who had been warned of their arrival but not the reason for it. As his long-standing employer, she had been the natural choice to identify the body, initially from a photograph, one they had found in a card folder along with several others of groups of people in evening dress. There was a date, written in pencil, on the back of each. They depicted the staff of Brockham's at their Christmas parties. In the centre was the man who had lain on the bed. 'Oughtn't the wife be the one to make the ID?' Brenda asked.

'If we can find her quickly. She might have emigrated, although we'll have to trace her, especially if they are still married. Go and speak to Carmen Brockham.' Ian sighed. He was hot and he was disturbed. Nothing quite like this had come his way before. It was vile and sickening. 'Eddie, you get cracking on finding Diane Graham.' DC Eddie Roberts was a new face in CID although known to them already. He had recently moved across from the uniformed branch but had fitted in instantly. A family man in his late thirties, he was affable and a willing worker. Ian had known immediately that he would be an easy person to get on with.

Brenda slid off the desk. Short's eyes dropped to her legs. She ignored his lasciviousness, she was used to it.

Ian returned to the three cardboard boxes in front of him. A scene-of-crime officer had declared them to have been untouched for some time, and they could therefore be removed from the house. The boxes were sealed with wide parcel tape and the film of dust on the top had shown them to have been undisturbed. They had brought them back to headquarters to go through. Graham had been an orderly man. The boxes contained bills and receipts stacked in chronological order but so far, apart from the marriage certificate in its original brown envelope, nothing of interest had turned up, certainly no divorce papers. As he glanced at the utility bills, all paid on time, Ian realised that the boxes were not the only thing undisturbed. There had been no forced entry, other than by PC Henderson and his colleague, and no sign that anything had been taken. But some-one had hated Graham enough to kill him while he was naked, and therefore more vulnerable, and then to mutilate him. And Malcolm Graham had presumably let that person in. Therefore it was someone he knew, someone, according to Talbot, he might have been expecting. The telephone company was already pre-paring a list of calls made from his number during the past month.

The next box contained credit card slips neatly attached to monthly accounts. Ian felt he was wasting his time, he might as well go home. The house-to-house team was doing the rounds in Frampton and would not be reporting back for some time. DC Campbell was still in the process of setting up the incident room in the village hall. Tomorrow they would concentrate on the staff at Brockham's where Graham had spent a large proportion of his life. But Frampton first. That was where he had lived and where he had died. Somebody had to know something.

Seven thirty. Ian sat up and massaged his back. He was inclined to slouch. The thought of sitting in his garden with a beer in his hand was tempting, but the least he could do was to finish examining the contents of the box he was going through. Once the job was out of the way, tomorrow would be free to concentrate on the house itself and the staff at Brockham's.

Half-way down the last box his fingers made contact with something slippery. From beneath a council tax bill, fully paid in one instalment, he pulled a photograph. The woman's beauty startled him, as did her nakedness. What was it doing there amongst the methodical filing of bills? And was it the clue they were looking for? Ian stared at the picture. The colours had faded a little and it was hard to say when it was taken. There were no clothes, therefore no fashion to suggest a year. The woman, girl really, stood in front of gold Dralon curtains, drawn across a wall or window. Her hair was dark brown, worn long and straight, but despite her beauty she looked uncomfortable.

She was in her mid to late teens. Ian looked more closely – she was possibly even younger.

But no, this wasn't a clue, that would be too easy. It was more likely to be Diane, Graham's wife, posing for one of those pictures some husbands like to take of their wives in the privacy of the bedroom.

'That's it. I'm off. If anyone needs me I can be found at home,' Ian told DC Eddie Roberts who was running his index finger down the page of a telephone directory. 'Get this copied. It might be the wife.' He handed him the photograph, which Eddie glanced at appreciatively.

The sky was no longer blue. A high, white dome which was not cloud but humidity arced over the town, entrapping the heat. Everywhere was a film of grit, spewed up from the gutters by traffic. Patches of lawn were yellow and scratchy but they would recover when it finally rained – which won't be tonight, Ian thought with regret. At least he was able to park almost outside his own house in Belmont Terrace, which was normally lined with cars, because some of his neighbours were away.

Inside number fourteen it was stuffy. The house had been closed up all day. Ian opened the windows and poured beer from the fridge. A note from Moira stood against the kettle. 'We're going on to the Italian. Have left you a salad. Love M,' it said. Long gone were the days when Moira stayed at home to look after him and Mark, when she cooked everything herself and there was pudding to follow. Still, he had lost weight and the food on the plate did look appetising beneath its protection of film even if the variety of mixed salads had come from plastic pots from Lavender's delicatessen in the High Street.

When Moira returned he was asleep. She sighed. Despite all his admonishments to her, he had left the kitchen window wide open.

Short was driving. Brenda, next to him, could smell his sweat. At least it wasn't as stale as on some days. They followed the Little Endesley road for about two miles then turned left into the driveway of Collerton Manor. Between banks of rhododendrons which had finished flowering the road was smooth and well maintained. The bushes gave way to a lawn unadorned by flower-beds. Surrounding it were tall trees and in the centre stood a stone sun-dial which threw its own long shadow across the grass.

'The Brockham millions,' Short said, impressed by the two-storey building ahead of him. 'Ten bedrooms, I'd bet, probably all en suite. Still, money can't buy you happiness.'

Brenda bowed her head and closed her eyes in resignation. Scruffy Short had managed the whole journey without uttering one cliché: that he would continue to do so had been too much to hope for.

Carmen Brockham was expecting them and had probably heard the car but she waited for them to ring the bell before coming to the door. Her eyes hardly seemed to waver but she gave them both a thorough once-over. 'You're very punctual', she said, turning to allow them inside. When she had shut the door she began to walk towards the back of the house. Brenda and Short followed.

The wide hallway was cool, the hard floor beneath their feet might well be genuine marble. Above the central staircase ran a three-sided gallery lined with closed doors. Brenda looked back and up. A chandelier hung on a chain from the rafters, and fanlights were set high in the front wall: it was like a scene from an old horror film. She shivered. It was not a happy house. It would cost a fortune to heat in winter but to Miss Brockham that would not be a problem.

They walked around one side of the sweeping staircase and out into the heat of the evening. What Carmen called the garden could more aptly have been described as grounds. There were no flowers there either. Instead three tiers of beautifully kept grass sloped down to the River Deben, visible through weeping willows, and upon which a pair of swans glided downstream. Beneath an oak tree stood three chairs and a wooden table; on it was a pitcher of something in which ice was melting. There were, John Short noticed with joy, three stemmed glasses. He turned to Brenda but she stared over his shoulder. Short had insisted upon driving because he was the sort of man who felt emasculated in the passenger seat beside a female. Tough luck, mate, she thought. You're going to be driving back as well.

'Are you allowed to drink?' Carmen raised the pitcher which glistened with condensation.

'I'd love one. Thank you', Brenda said quickly, 'but Inspector Short is driving.'

As they sat in the shade of the tree Brenda did not know what to make of the stunning woman whom she had heard so much about but had never actually met. Her short hair was blonde with paler highlights, neither of which was her natural colour. Her eyebrows were dark, her skin olive. Through newspaper articles they knew her age to be forty-six but money and lack of stress had combined to keep her young. Not even a husband to consider, Brenda realised. Carmen had been sunbathing. Beneath the halter-neck top of a patterned kaftan affair, the straps of a turquoise bikini were showing. It was skimpy. When she turned, the curved sides of her breasts could be seen, paler than the rest of her skin.

Brenda accepted a drink, not caring what Short might say afterwards. Her throat was parched. She took a sip of the icy liquid. Whatever it was it had a kick.

'You wanted to discuss Mr Graham,' Carmen began as she filled her own glass. 'Is there a problem at Brockham's?' She said the name as if she was unconnected with it.

'Not that we know of.' Short tugged at his moustache and tried not to ogle the woman. 'Is Malcolm Graham in this photograph?' He held out the picture of the firm's annual party taken the previous December.

'Yes. That's Malcolm.' She pointed to the man in the centre. Her hand shook.

'Miss Brockham, I'm afraid we have bad news. Mr Graham is dead.' Both he and Brenda watched closely for her reaction. The sides of her mouth quivered, a smothered smile or a nervous reaction.

'Dead? But I had no idea he was ill.' The response was a beat too late.

'He was murdered.'

'My God.' Her hand jerked involuntarily as she replaced her glass on the table. The shock seemed genuine but beneath the tree with the shifting pattern of leaves dappling her face it was hard to tell. 'Do they know at the store?'

'No. We needed a positive identification and we thought you should know first. Sylvia Harris contacted us when Mr Graham failed to turn up for work,' Brenda replied.

'Ah, Sylvie. Yes, she would.'

'We'll need to talk to everyone at Brockham's and, with your permission, on the premises.'

'Naturally. I'll have a room set aside for you.' Carmen stood. 'I'm so sorry, Inspector, you have no drink. Do let me fetch you some fresh orange juice.'

'She needs time. I wonder why?' Brenda said as their hostess walked slowly towards the house. 'And did you see that odd look on her face?'

But when she returned, ice clinking in the glass, Carmen seemed worried, as if something disturbing had crossed her mind. 'I suppose you're going to ask if I can think of anyone who disliked him. I can't. He wasn't an easy man to know but Malcolm was invaluable to me and much respected by the staff. Urbane is the word I would use to decribe him. However, his private life was not my concern so I can't help you there. He was loyal, too much so for his own good. I doubt he would've taken holidays had I not insisted.'

'Any idea where he went, or who with? Girlfriend, that sort of thing?'

'No. No idea. Perhaps he stayed at home. As for women, he's never mentioned anyone in particular.'

Strange, Short was thinking. They had, however obliquely, shared two decades of their adult life and she claims to know nothing about him. Liar, liar, pants on fire, he quoted silently, briefly enjoying a picture of Carmen Brockham dressed in nothing else but tiny white pants. 'Several women maybe?' Short persisted. Carmen Brockham was being a little vague.

'I really couldn't say.'

'He didn't even mention his wife?'

Carmen frowned. 'He doesn't have a wife. Even I know that much. He's been with me for twenty-one years and this is the first I've heard of it.' This time the response was genuine. 'I think you must be mistaken. He's not . . .'

'He's not what?'

Carmen shook her head. 'I think what I mean is that he's terribly set in his ways. Look, I'll speak to Sylvia Harris this evening and get her to arrange somewhere private for you to conduct your interviews. She prefers to be called Sylvie, by the way. Oh, am I allowed to tell anyone?'

Short did not hesitate. 'Only Mrs Harris. And please make it clear to her that she is to discuss this with no one. If she does we'll charge her with obstruction.' A bit strong but the woman might be a gossip.

'I understand. I suppose you'll have to search Malcolm's house. I mean – well, I assume that's the procedure?'

Neither Short nor Brenda answered. It was a bizarre question, one which suggested that Miss Brockham hoped they wouldn't have to search it. She was nervous now and there could be little doubt that she knew far more about her employee than she was saying. They got up to leave, Carmen standing belatedly. On the way back through the house they came across a youngish woman who stepped aside for them. One of the staff, presumably, as Carmen told her she was free to leave.

'What did you make of that little lot? I'm buggered, is all I can say.'

'Very prescient, Inspector,' Brenda replied as they got into the car.

'Can you come up with anything better, my lovely?'

Brenda couldn't. Malcolm Graham remained an enigma, but one who had inspired hatred. The Talbots had been truthful but Carmen Brockham had lied when she said she hardly knew the man. It would be interesting to hear what the staff at the store thought of him.

'Good-looking woman. Nice pair of tits. You don't get many of those to the pound.'

Oh, spare me, please, Brenda thought as they began the drive back.

Over an hour later, tired at the end of a long day and still reeling from what she had witnessed earlier, Brenda left for home. She almost turned left at the roundabout on Saxborough Road to return to the dismal terraced property in which she had lived with her husband until, as she had done with him, she had finally got shot of it. Ahead lay the coast and Andrew, so gentle and understanding, and the beautiful house she had not yet had time to adjust to and accept as her home. With all that to return to she felt the tension draining away and the events of the day falling into perspective.

7

Carmen was alone. She had heard Sandy drive off earlier. Sandy was one of the four house staff she employed. She had watched the police car pull away, walked back to the house and shut the front door, then leant on it for support because she was no longer able to control the trembling in her limbs.

It was ten minutes before she returned to the garden and refilled her glass. The air was still and heavy, there was no longer a trace of breeze to ruffle the leaves of the tree. She sat beneath it anyway and poured the remains of the pitcher into her glass, filling it to the brim and slopping it over the top. It did not matter that the ice had all melted and the martini was now warm.

Malcolm was dead. She felt relief, not regret, at the news. There was no need to face him now, no need to worry any more, except for one small thing – what the police might find and what it might do to Neil if it came out. But would the police make the connection? It was all so long ago. I'll sacrifice my happiness, the rest of my life if I have to, she thought, if it means saving his reputation. She meant it and, knowing that and what it would do to her if she lost him, scalding tears ran down her face.

Half an hour later the drink had had the desired anaesthetising effect and she swayed a little as she went towards the house. This slight lack of control was exceptional, but it had been an exceptional day. Her father's drinking habits had filled her with disgust, she could never become like him.

The sun was beginning to set. The lengthening shadows of the horse chestnuts fell across the smooth lawns and rainbow colours danced in the spray from the automatic sprinklers which were timed to come on at nine. It was time to make that call to Sylvie.

In the high-ceilinged lounge she sat on one of the cream leather settees, the telephone beside her, its lead trailing over the floor to beneath the table upon which it usually stood. Her call was answered swiftly, as if Sylvie had been waiting for it. 'Hello, Sylvie. It's me. Carmen. The police were here this evening.'

'About Malcolm? It was me who contacted them. He didn't turn up for work this morning. He's always so punctual that I knew something had to be wrong. Have you heard anything? Is he all right?'

'I wish you'd contacted me after you rang the police.'

'I . . . oh. I'm sorry, Carmen. I see now that I ought to have done.'

Carmen sighed. At least she was spared confronting Malcolm, but if Sylvie had rung her first she could have offered to go to the house herself. But then I might have found his body, she realised. Besides, Sylvie acted rashly during times of stress, it probably hadn't occurred to her to ring her employer. 'He couldn't come in,' she said quietly. 'He's dead. Murdered, in fact.'

The shocked silence lasted several seconds. 'How?'

Carmen frowned. She had not thought to ask. 'I don't know.'

'Not suicide?'

What was the matter with Sylvie? She was normally cold and efficient and she, more than anyone, would know Malcolm would never take his own life. Tonight she sounded desperate. 'Suicide? Malcolm? Are you mad?' Carmen did not want to prolong the conversation. 'Look, they want to interview everyone at the store tomorrow. Would you do me a favour and make the staff room available – no one's to use it until the police have finished. Oh, and Sylvie, they said to tell you that you're not to discuss it. In fact, the Inspector threatened to charge you if you did. Don't worry, I'm sure it was an idle threat, but not a word, okay?'

'Of course not. Will you be coming in yourself tomorrow?'

'No. I've already told them all I can.'

'Carmen, did you mean what you said about me taking over from Malcolm?'

'Did I say that?' Yes, perhaps she had mentioned it casually, but that was some years ago, before she knew Sylvie Harris really well. Efficient she might be but it was in her nature to antagonise the staff if she was given complete control. Malcolm had always managed to keep her in her place. Just. 'Well, it's still too early to make any such decision. The poor man's hardly cold. Goodnight, Sylvie.' Carmen replaced the receiver but not before she had heard the disappointed gasp on the other end of the line which made her feel mean.

As she walked from room to room, the cork heels of her mules echoed in her wake. Her friends told her the house was too large for one person. Carmen did not think so. She enjoyed the space and solitude and it had been in the family for three generations, although with her death would come the end of the line. There would be no children now.

The thought of the food Sandy had prepared and left for her nauseated her. She would have made another jug of martini except it would be against all her principles and she needed a clear head. There had to be a way out of this. It would come to her if she concentrated hard enough. She continued to walk, biting the side of her mouth in frustration as she did so. There was also the problem of Sylvie. Better to have her on her side, especially if she had been the one to write those anonymous letters. Yes, she would have to let her down lightly but she could certainly give her a pay rise.

DC Eddie Roberts looked nothing like Alan Campbell. He was of middle height and weight, a shambling sort of man with floppy brown hair and a ready smile. His life had been happy, uneventful apart from the birth of his children, and fulfilling. But he and Alan shared one thing in common, single-mindedness. Both men, given a task, would follow it through to the end, refusing to give up until they had a satisfactory answer. Alan made use of computers and endless cross-referencing, Eddie tended to use his brain, the telephone and the contacts he had picked up over the years. In this instance his answer lay in logic. He simply made a plausible guess, that Mrs Malcolm Graham might have reverted to her maiden name. He picked up the local telephone directory and found several numbers listed under the name Hicks. There was a D. Hicks who lived in Saxborough. He dialled the ten digits and was rewarded immediately. The woman to whom he was speaking was Malcolm Graham's wife, or ex-wife. He did not ask, that could wait. 'We think you might be able to help us with a case we're investigating,' he said after

51

explaining who he was and clarifying her own identification. 'Would it be possible to speak to you this evening?' The photograph the Chief had given him lay on the desk. It might be that of the woman to whom he was speaking.

She agreed without asking a single question. Perhaps she knows he's dead already, Eddie thought. Perhaps she did the deed herself.

DCI Roper had left the building and gone home, Campbell was over at Frampton, and Brenda and Short had not yet returned from Collerton Manor. He would wait until they did so before setting off himself although it was too optimistic to hope that his journey would not be necessary. 'Will somewhere between nine and nine thirty be convenient?'

'It's rather late, but it'll have to be, I suppose,' Diane Hicks replied sullenly.

He hung up, wondering why she had stayed so close. If Eddie ever decided to leave to make a new start, not that he ever would, he would at least choose another county in which to do so. Family, maybe. Her mother or sisters are in the area, he decided. It was not unnatural for Eddie Roberts to think that way. His house was always full of relatives, his or his wife's, a fact which seemed not to bother him at all.

Eddie made copies of the photograph and studied it. It could have been taken at any time – the long, straight hair was dateless – and there was also the chance that the nude girl might not have been known to Graham. Just because it had been in his possession did not mean he had held the camera. Nor did it mean he had known it was there at all. He might have scooped it up from elsewhere with his papers. He was too meticulous a man to have shoved it away anyhow.

There were voices in the corridor. Short and Brenda had returned. The three of them sat in the general office, coffees in front of them, as Brenda outlined their impression of Carmen Brockham and the conversation which had taken place. 'It's the usual story,' she said. 'She knows of no one who wished him harm, she doesn't know him other than through work, and he was hardworking and loyal.' She counted the points off on her fingers. 'And she's glad he's dead. Not that she said so in words.'

Eddie had whistled. 'Did she do it?'

'I'd say she was capable,' Short had answered. 'She asked if we needed to search his house.'

'Pretty obvious we'd have to. I wonder what she doesn't want us to find, unless it's her fingerprints all over the shop. Hang on, this isn't her, is it?' Eddie slid copies of the Polaroid shot towards them.

'No,' Short said glancing at it briefly. 'We're off home.'

Brenda gave him two minutes then left herself. She had had enough of Short for one day without having to chat to him in the car-park.

It was later than Eddie had anticipated. He did not leave headquarters until almost nine, taking a WPC with him. Mrs Graham, or Diane Hicks, might not have lived with her husband for a very long time but there was no knowing how she would take the news of his death.

'Great start to the week,' Eddie commented once they were in the car and on their way. 'I said I'd be home early. My kids won't recognise me soon.'

'Neither will mine.' Janice Clarke grinned at the surprise on the DC's face as he glanced at her quickly. So many of them forgot it was that much harder for a woman with a family in the job.

They discussed their children until they arrived on the outskirts of the university town of Saxborough, some seventeen miles from Rickenham Green, then they concentrated upon finding the right address.

Diane Hicks knew they were coming but seemed unprepared for their visit. She answered the door in a pink towelling bathrobe. Her feet were encased in worn slippers and her face was shiny with moisturiser. No, Eddie Roberts realised, not unprepared, quite the opposite. She was making a statement: it's late and I'm ready for bed. You can't stay long. Interesting.

In his pocket Eddie had the photograph found amongst Graham's papers but even allowing for the intervening years, which had not been kind to his wife, it could not have been her.

'You'd better come in,' she said ungraciously, leading them into the sitting-room which was tidy but characterless. 'I can't imagine why you think I'd be able to help you.'

'It's about Malcolm Graham,' Eddie began. There were two

53

wedding photographs on the sideboard. Different brides but similar in looks, presumably Diane's daughters. But were they also Graham's daughters?

'Oh, him.'

No love lost there, Eddie thought. 'When did you last see him, Mrs Graham?'

'Miss Hicks. I thought you knew that I use that name, that's how you found me, or so you said. I reverted to my maiden name on the day that I left him in 1974. I haven't set eyes on him since. Nor have I wanted to. Why? What's he done?'

'He's dead, Miss Hicks.'

'I see.' No emotion showed on her face but she reached into the pocket of her robe, withdrew a packet of cigarettes and lit one with a match. 'Did he suffer?'

'I, um ...' Eddie was not sure what she meant by the question.

'Was he ill? An accident? What?'

'He was murdered.'

'Oh.' She paused. 'I see. And you think I killed him. I would've done if he'd ever come near me. But, no, I didn't. Did he leave a will?'

The woman was merciless. 'We don't know that yet.'

'I never knew if he made one when we were together, he always refused to discuss such matters.' She sighed. 'I brought the children up on my own, he didn't contribute a penny. They were eight and seven when I walked out and there were none of these so-called agencies around then to chase men up for money.' She paused. When she spoke again she was honest enough to admit that she hadn't wanted his money, that she wouldn't have taken it under any circumstances. 'It's different now, though. I feel I've earned it. We're not divorced, you see. At first I didn't want to give him the chance to put some other woman through it. He would have to have waited the full five years in those days. I thought he'd eventually divorce me, but he didn't.'

'Miss Hicks, may I ask you why you left him?'

She sighed. 'He was shiftless and idle. He never settled in any job for long. He was always saying he wasn't appreciated or he deserved more money, that one day he'd show them all. He always seemed to care more for the bloody garden than he did

54

for me and he took no interest in the children. All in all he was a boring, boorish man.' She turned away to find an ashtray but Eddie realised it was to avoid showing her embarrassment when she added, 'He used to hit me, and sometimes the girls. They've not seen him since that day either, and they have no wish to.' Her face coloured and she patted her hair in an almost girlish gesture. 'He also had disgusting habits in the bedroom.' Eddie raised his eyebrows. 'You surely don't want me to describe them?' She looked shocked.

'No. No, that won't be necessary.' But some sort of pattern was emerging. The man put on one face at work and to his neighbours but his murder certainly seemed to have been sexually motivated. There was the nude photograph and now this. Eddie wondered if there was more to come, if Malcolm Graham had done more than hit his daughters and that had been the reason Diane Hicks had stood it no longer and had left him.

'I can't tell you any more than that. If you speak to my daughters they'll say the same. They've children of their own who've never seen their grandfather. How did he die?' It was an afterthought, her tone implying she didn't care.

'He was, uh, stabbed.' She need not know more just yet.

'Then whoever killed him was a woman and I hope he did suffer.'

'What makes you say that?' Did Diane Hicks already know the circumstances of his death?

'Because he was different around men. It was only weaker people, women and children, upon whom he preyed. He was a bully, you see.'

'Did you know he was still in the area? He worked at Brockham's in Rickenham Green for twenty-one years.'

Diane lit another cigarette and shrugged. 'No, I didn't know that. I don't use the place, I shop here or in Ipswich. But if you're trying to tell me he'd changed, then you're wrong. He might have held down a job in the end but men like that never change. I'm tired, Constable Roberts. If you'll excuse me, I'd like to go to bed now.'

They had been dismissed. Janice Clarke had not been needed to provide a shoulder to soak up Diane's tears but Eddie had still been glad of her presence. The ex-Mrs Graham was a vindictive woman and she had been wearing only her nightclothes.

*   *   *

Alan Campbell remained in the red-brick village hall until he was totally satisfied that all the equipment was in working order. During the late afternoon and early evening he had been grateful that the roof was tiled and not constructed of sheets of corrugated iron, as it had once been his misfortune to suffer in similar circumstances in baking heat. The building was cool, the window where he sat shaded by the trees which lined the perimeter of a playing-field. Alan waited patiently for the first team on house-to-house inquiries to report back. He would then feed the salient points of their findings into the computer, and he was looking forward to it now that the engineers had gone and he was linked up.

By now there would be talk in the village and most people would have come to the right conclusion, although they would not know the gruesome details. It couldn't be helped, a murder investigation could not be conducted in secrecy.

Alan got up to make tea, banishing all thoughts of Helen from his mind, not liking to imagine that she might come to an equally violent end through her chosen line of work.

DC Roberts had rung through earlier to say that they'd found the wife and he was on his way to see her, and that someone was about to fax through copies of a photograph. 'We've had the original doctored by the blokes in the lab, head and shoulders shots only now. Get them shown around the village. We don't know who the woman is, see if anyone there does.'

The machine began to spew out paper. Alan closed his eyes. The first half a dozen copies were of the original photographs for police use only. These were followed by the head shots. The whole world's sick, he thought as he looked at the the nude. Why couldn't more people be decent and solid like Eddie Roberts?

It was after eleven when he handed over. If the half of the population of the village who had known Malcolm Graham was to be believed, he was, to use Inspector Short's jargon, a paragon of virtue, a pillar of society. Inspector Short would also have loved the clichéd phrases contained in the reports: 'A lovely man, wouldn't hurt a fly.' 'Always polite and helpful.' 'Couldn't do enough for charity.' 'He judged the baby show at the summer fair once. You should've seen him, he was a natural with children.' 'You wanted to know anything about gardening you only had to ask that man. Never known anyone with such green fingers.' And so it went on. Alan found it almost as sickening as what they had discovered that morning. Maybe these people were superstitious and did not want to bad-mouth a dead man but the truth was that Graham came across as too good to be true. And in the world DC Alan Campbell had had to come to recognise, there was no such thing.

8

Sylvie Harris was agitated throughout the whole of Tuesday as she began to suspect that the responsibility of Malcolm's job might be too much for her. Added to that was the fact that at least two members of staff were missing at any given time. Four officers had arrived, albeit inconspicuously, and she had had to find another room for the second pair. 'This way,' she had said, shepherding the first pair of detectives into the lift and leaving immediately she had shown them into the staff room. The others were using Malcolm's office. Now she hurried from one department to another, helping out behind a till if necessary and dealing with inquiries from customers. She was hot and flustered and did not know how the auburn-haired WDC managed to look so cool and unruffled.

Brenda had watched the woman hurry away then glanced around their accommodation. Situated at the top of the building, the staff room had barred windows and a view of rooftops upon which pigeons sunned themselves. The furnishings were adequate but had been there since a previous era. The two sofas and several armchairs made the setting informal but the only alternative was to sit around the gate-legged table in the high-backed chairs like a group of students. 'Where do we start?' she asked as she stared at the numerous names on the lists in front of her. Eddie Roberts and another detective constable had been provided with an equally long list. There were many more staff than they had imagined, taking into account the ones behind the scenes, the office and catering staff, security and cleaners.

John Short was peering into a cupboard, one hand on the door knob, the other scratching his behind. 'From the beginning,' he answered without turning around. Having found nothing more interesting than a couple of rusted biscuit tins and a container of dried skimmed milk, he shut the cupboard door again. Short consulted the list and reached for the telephone which stood on the table. The names of the personnel were grouped together by department. He dialled the internal number for Ladies' Fashions and asked the first of the staff to come up.

Both sash windows were open to their full extent, which despite the bars was no more than six inches. It appeared that Brockham's were taking no chances on anyone falling out or committing suicide. The sun streamed through the dirty panes and a pigeon cooed on the ledge. 'This is a waste of time,' Short muttered at a quarter to twelve as they waited for the next person to arrive. He wiped his brow with a crumpled blue handkerchief.

'Oh, I don't know.' Brenda studied her notebook. True, no one had been very forthcoming but it was hardly surprising. Malcolm Graham had visited each section once a day to check there were no problems but didn't stay long enough to chat. A pointless exercise, someone had remarked, as Sylvie Harris was always at hand to sort things out. No one claimed to really know Malcolm, he was just someone who was always there and to whom they could turn if there was a serious problem. Pleasantries would be exchanged but there had never been any of that sharing of personal details which occurred between staff working together on the same floor. Polite and pleasant, was the general consensus so far.

'What do you mean?'

'They've all said much the same thing, but you could tell there's a divided opinion. Some of them were indifferent, even when they heard he was dead, others were shocked and sorry and one or two, although they didn't say so, obviously disliked the man.'

'Yes, thank you, Brenda. Even I could see that. But it's normal in a place like this. There are so many people and you can't be liked by everyone.'

'I disagree. If he was such an anonymous figure, if he only ever made small talk, how could he have been disliked?'

Before Short could answer there was a timid knock on the door. 'Come in,' he said. Audrey Hepburn, in *Breakfast at*

58

Tiffany's, he thought immediately Elaine Pritchard entered the room. Certainly the same figure and bone structure, the gamin features and wistful expression. 'Take a seat, Mrs Pritchard.' He tried not to stare at her legs.

'Thank you.' Her voice was low but perfectly clear.

'I expect you realise the reason for these interviews.'

'Yes. Mr Graham's dead.'

'His death was not accidental. Can you think of any reason why anyone here might have wished him any harm?'

She shook her head. 'No. As far as I can tell none of us knew much about him, except maybe Mrs Harris who worked closely with him. I'm afraid we've talked about nothing else since we heard. He was sort of . . .' She shrugged. 'I don't know. It's hard to explain.'

'Part of the furniture?'

Brenda sniffed. The seventh cliché of the morning. She'd been counting.

'Yes. Someone you saw every day without really thinking about.'

'And your own feelings towards Mr Graham?'

'I didn't have any.'

Brenda glanced up. It was a strange sort of answer, negative, yet very definite. 'None?' she asked, smiling to soften the suspicion in her voice.

'None whatsoever. He did me a favour by moving me from Lighting to Cosmetics, but that was because he knew I'd do well there. It wasn't anything personal, just a business move.'

'How long have you worked here, Mrs Pritchard?' Short was speaking again.

'About six months.'

'Who employed you?'

'Mr Graham.'

'I see. And were you badly in need of a job?'

Elaine's smile was gentle. 'No. Not at all. I'd already got one. I just fancied a change and, to be honest, the pay here is a few pounds a week more than I was earning.'

'So Mr Graham interviewed you?'

'Mrs Harris initially, then she sent me along to see him. He had the final say, apparently. I was with him no more than ten minutes. He seemed satisfied and said they'd let me know within a week. They did, and here I am.'

John Short was bored with asking the same questions and receiving similar answers. He asked his final one, having decided it was lunchtime and that the garden of the Three Feathers would be graced by his presence within a very short length of time. 'How did he treat the staff? I mean, was there any difference between how he dealt with males and females?' They needed a sexual connection, no matter how tenuous.

Elaine chewed her lip. With her back to the window Short could not be certain but he thought she looked paler. 'None whatsoever. If there had been, there would've been complaints from the girls and he'd never have been allowed to work here for so long. Carmen Brockham insists on professional behaviour from all of her staff.'

Interesting, Short thought. A vehement answer, that one, and so far Mrs Pritchard was the only one of them to have mentioned their real boss. 'Thank you. That's all we need for now.' He watched her walk to the door then open and close it behind her with dignity.

'The Feathers calls, my beauty,' he said, standing up stiffly. 'Must be your round.'

'You're beginning to sound like the Chief. Besides, I'm not into all this equality stuff.'

Short snorted. 'You invented it, Gibbons. You were born on the wrong continent. You should've been a bloody Amazon. Come on, let's not waste precious drinking time.'

They walked the length of the upper floor, which was busier now that it was lunchtime. Those who worked elsewhere were doing their shopping whilst they had a chance. Then they rode down on the escalators beneath the rows of tiny white bulbs which decorated them and stepped into the cosmetics department. Beautiful faces advertising lipsticks pouted at them from posters and the air was heady with a mixture of scents. Before they reached the main doors to the High Street Brenda stopped at a glass counter, picked up a bottle and sniffed, then sprayed perfume on to her wrists. John Short stared at her. 'Well, why not? They're testers. That's what they're there for,' she told him. 'And it's my favourite.'

'Well, if you're very good and help me solve this case I'll buy you some.'

'And pigs might fly,' Brenda retorted before she was aware of what she was saying. The Chief's right, she thought, red-faced, as they walked up the High Street. Short's way of speaking is contagious.

They pushed open the wrought-iron gate at the side of the pub and chose a table. It had clouded over and there was a slight breeze but it was still warm enough to sit outside because the garden of the Three Feathers was an enclosed area of paving which attracted the heat. Around the sides were half-dead plants in cracked pots. Brenda decided they had suffocated from the smell of creosote from the fencing which had recently been treated. But inside was worse. Ceiling fans whirred slowly and ineffectively over the worn plush furnishings. The combined smells of smoke and fried food added to the oppressive heat of the bar but did not deter the regulars who sat with glasses of beer and plates of unappetising food in front of them.

'Get me some peanuts, will you?' Short called from the doorway.

The juke-box clamoured into life just as Brenda was about to order their drinks. Short could not hear the words she muttered in his direction. She carried their glasses outside, the packet of peanuts between her teeth.

'I wonder if Eddie's come up with anything?' Brenda hoped the other team had had more success than they had.

'Same as us, I bet.' Short sucked beer foam from the straggly ends of his moustache. 'Bugger all.'

'Sylvie Harris is on our list. She must know something about him. She's been his deputy for heaven knows how long. And she was worried enough to call us immediately.'

'Perhaps she did it. Maybe she was after his job and did him in because she couldn't wait until he retired.'

Short had been joking but Brenda saw it as a possibility. People had killed for less. 'You might be right.' She sipped her Campari and soda. 'Elaine Pritchard didn't seem to think much of him either.'

John Short shrugged and stuffed some peanuts into his mouth. Crumbs and salt attached themselves to his moustache. Then he stopped chewing. 'What was it she said, about the Brockham woman?'

'That she expected professional behaviour from all her staff.'

'Yes, but our Mrs Pritchard was adamant that there was no suggestion of hanky-panky. There has to be a sexual element in it somewhere and if the delicious, melon-breasted Carmen Brockham has made a point of stressing professionalism, then maybe she's had cause to, maybe Mr Goody-Two-Shoes Graham hasn't always been quite the paragon of virtue he now appears. Maybe he used to touch up the staff. Well, we know he's got some nasty little ways. If what his wife said was true then our man was a bit of a bastard.'

'Oh, for God's sake, will you talk English?'

'Pardon?'

Brenda sighed deeply and shook her head. He doesn't even know he's doing it. Accept it, girl, he isn't going to change. 'Nothing. Forget it.'

'I will if you get the next round as well. And that's no way to talk to an inspector if you're after promotion, my girl.' But he was grinning. He enjoyed irritating Brenda, but it was his turn to buy the drinks. He stood up and fumbled in his pocket for money. 'But you're magnificent when you're angry' he called to her as he made his way towards the bar.

Brenda closed her eyes and bit her lip, but she was laughing too.

By three o'clock on Tuesday afternoon the forensic team had finished at Malcolm Graham's house. They left with their little bags of fibres and threads and carpet sweepings. Fingerprint dust lay over everything: the neat precision of Malcolm's life had been obliterated. Upstairs, the bedding had been removed from the main bedroom along with all his clothes. They were taken away for analysis.

Ian exchanged a few words with the officer on the door then, with a pang, entered the house, remembering what had awaited him the last time. Eddie Roberts was at his side. Another detective constable had relieved him at Brockham's half-way through the morning. Ian had wanted someone whose methods he knew when he started the search. 'We'll begin in the living-room,' he said. Together they entered it. Already it had acquired the aura of a room no longer used. Maybe I'm being fanciful, Ian thought, but each time I go to a property where a death has taken place it's as if the house has died along with the person. 'Start on the sideboard,' Ian said. 'I'll check the bureau.' But the bureau turned out to be a drinks cabinet, artfully disguised. The drawers beneath the flap were not drawers, but a cupboard containing glasses. The sideboard held nothing but table linen, unused for years judging by the yellowed edges of the folds.

The kitchen was tidy; tinned goods were lined up behind sliding doors, bread, now stale, was in the bin, and a reasonable selection of healthy food lay on shelves in the fridge. In the small dining-room nothing was to be found other than a polished table and four chairs, giving the impression that it was rarely used.

The bathroom could only have belonged to a man. It was minimalistic, almost spartan, but still pleasing to the eye. It was decorated in black and white with chrome trimmings. Clean white towels hung over rails which could be heated and lightly scented soap lay in a dish. The cabinet over the sink was almost empty: razor, shaving foam, toothbrush and paste, four bottles of after-shave, a small container of aspirin and antihistamine cream which could be bought over the counter. Not a prescription medicine in sight.

'It's like the man didn't bloody exist,' Ian swore. There was nothing in these rooms which gave away what made him tick. 'Come on, just the bedrooms left now.'

There was a large built-in cupboard in the main bedroom at the back of the house. It had held clothes and shoes and was now empty apart from two travelling bags on the top shelf next to which the boxes of receipts had been stored. They, too, were empty. Maybe he did go away, Ian thought, despite what Carmen Brockham had told Brenda and Short.

And, lastly, the spare room. Not a bedroom, this, more of an office. Ian felt a surge of hope. Why would Malcolm Graham have needed an office at home when he had a large one of his own at work? On a plain desk stood an old word processor. Someone else would have to deal with that. Ian wasn't sure he could even switch it on. He had been forced to have a computer on his desk at the station and was able to tap in three simple instructions, but the rest of its functions might not have existed. Alan Campbell was the man for the job.

DC Eddie Roberts had hardly spoken. He pulled open a drawer of the desk and frowned. 'Diskettes, sir. All labelled with numbers but nothing to say what's on them.'

'Can you work this thing?' Ian indicated the word processor.

'It's a bit of a relic but I can probably manage.' Eddie plugged it in, switched it on and cleared the screen before sliding in the diskette numbered 'One', printed as a word not a numeral. When he pressed the code key and a number the menu appeared. 'Recall from disk, sir, I think that's what we want.' Eddie shook his head. 'Sorry. I assumed the word One was the file name. It isn't. He must have a key or a code somewhere.' But there were no disks which suggested this to be the case.

'Perhaps he's written it down somewhere,' Ian suggested, knowing that he would have done so to save himself embarrassment. But there was nothing to be found in the other drawers apart from stationery.

'You'll have to get Alan on to it, sir.'

'Yes. Forget the sir while we're here, Eddie. Right, what've we got here?'

As in the main bedroom, a built-in wardrobe had been fitted. This one contained another cardboard box. It had been finger-printed, which meant that Forensics knew it had been handled recently. Ian lifted the lid. Cheque-book stubs and paying-in books. Yes, Graham would have needed to go to it each time a book ran out. It would be taken away and examined. An expensive briefcase, now battered, sat on the floor. 'Empty,' Ian said in exasperation. 'What sort of a man are we dealing with? Eddie, I . . .' He stopped. Eddie Roberts, his back towards him, was motionless, staring at something which Ian couldn't see. 'What is it?'

'I wondered what was wrong.' He tapped the back of the cupboard. 'Take a look from the side. The wardrobe's not as deep. It doesn't go all the way to the wall.'

'False back?'

'You bet.'

But neither man could find a way to get into it. They tapped and prodded but could not find a lever or button.

'Let's get some tools.'

These were found in the garage, clean and dry in a tool-box. Eddie chose a large chisel. 'It's plywood. One smash and we're through then I can lever the wood out.'

'A bit drastic, don't you think?'

'What would you suggest?'

'Quite. Well, carry on then.' Ian winced as Eddie wielded the first blow and the wood shattered. He wrenched away the panels. 'And now we have it,' he said with satisfaction when the shelves came into view. There was a camera, developing and printing chemicals and another cardboard box. Ian took it out and dumped it on the floor. Photographs. All nude females in various poses, some more suggestive than others, but no two the same. And most of them were of young girls.

Both men were silent for several seconds. It was Eddie who spoke first. 'Perhaps we should get someone other than Alan to deal with the word processor.'

'Yes.' They were both thinking the same thing. No way could Alan Campbell, having witnessed – in front of his colleagues at the station – his own wife appearing in blue films, be allowed to match up what were probably the names and details of the women who were in those pictures. 'You're right. It's probably best to leave him where he is.'

Half an hour later ominous clouds loomed over the horizon and they were on their way back to the station. There seemed to be little doubt now that the motive was sexual and, if they were really lucky, they might now have a photograph of Malcolm Graham's killer in their possession.

A pleasant breeze caught at the ends of Jane Stevenson's short dark bob as she drove to work on Tuesday morning with the driver's window open. The humidity was lower, too, making the air seem fresher even in rush hour traffic. In the distance, way beyond the rooftops of Rickenham Green, the cloudless sky was paler, almost white with a slight yellow tinge. Jane felt easier. She and George had talked. He had admitted he had a problem, no more than that, no solutions, but at least it was a start.

The locks had been changed and the credit cards cancelled. Jane put the loss of her handbag down to experience. The police had not come back to her, but she had never supposed that they would.

By midday clouds had formed. At first they were small and perfectly white. Soon they were joined by larger, greyer ones. Raining or not, I must go to Brockham's at lunchtime, Jane told herself as she filled in yet another form.

With no idea what to buy for her daughter-in-law's birthday she strolled around the ground floor of the department store looking at perfume and toiletry sets. Until she had had the baby, clothes were out of the question. A woman of roughly the same age was staring at her, at first with a puzzled expression then with a smile, but she turned away to serve a customer just as Jane realised who she was. I'll pop in again, she thought, realising how much time she had already wasted and there was her sandwich to eat when she got back. With only a few minutes to spare she bought some perfume, paying more than she had intended but Emma had not had an easy pregnancy. A bit of luxury would cheer her up.

By four o'clock all the lights in the Social Security building were on and the first spots of rain hit the pavement. Condensation formed on the ill-fitting windows and the waiting area smelled of damp clothing. When it was time to leave Jane stepped outside, bare-headed and with only a cotton jacket for protection. She glanced at the Coach and Horses over the road then hurried down to the underground car-park. 'You carry on if it does you good,' George had said to her. But the attraction of that single drink after work had gone. She was not sure whether it was because it was no longer a secret or if Friday night's experience had anything to do with it.

Jane parked in the road and let herself into the house. George was in the kitchen. A worried frown pulled down the corners of his mouth. She had come to hate that expression. 'What is it, George?' she asked impatiently, not wanting to hear the answer, not wanting to hear he'd had another bad day.

'Your handbag.' He pointed to the worktop.

'What?' She turned around and saw it. The leather was sodden and therefore darker.

'When it started to rain heavily I went out to tie up the clematis. You know I've been meaning to do it. The bag was on the back door handle.'

66

Jane nodded. Both of them had meant to tidy up the plant for ages. The back yard had a fence and a small raised border on one side and the blank wall of a neighbour's extension on the other. Two years ago the clematis had been planted in a tub in the hope of disguising the ugly red bricks. It had suddenly shot up and needed securing. Heavy rain would have broken the still delicate tendrils. 'Did you look inside it?'

'Of course not, love. You know I wouldn't do that.'

Nervously she opened the flap. Nothing was missing. 'I don't understand it.' She held out the open wallet. 'Even the money's still here.'

'All of it?'

'Yes.'

George ran a hand through his light brown hair. 'Well, someone must've had a fit of conscience or else picked it up by mistake and was too ashamed to bring it to the door.'

Jane knew the latter was unlikely. 'I'd better let the police know.' She dialled the station and quoted the case number she had been given; after being told that the officers concerned would be informed she was thanked for her trouble. 'They didn't seem very surprised,' she told George. 'Maybe they thought I'd made it all up. Look, why don't we go out? I'd written off the money, we might as well spend some of it.'

Jane was smiling. It took years off her age and George saw the woman she had been before his illness had worn her down. He could not refuse her.

'I saw Elaine Pritchard today,' she said as they drove back into town. 'She's working in Brockham's now. She looks a lot better than when we last saw her.'

But George wasn't really listening. He was still thinking about the handbag and its intact contents.

It was late when they returned. Not having an answering-machine they did not know that their number had been ringing at regular intervals and, not expecting any calls, they did not bother to dial 1471. If Emma had gone into premature labour their son would have kept on trying all night if he had to.

At last the multi-coloured flags which were strung in diagonals over the forecourt began to stir. The plastic triangles which had dangled flaccid and soft in the heat for weeks now snapped in the breeze. A wisp of cloud broke the uniform blue of the sky.

Roger Pender strolled outside, fingering his neat moustache. He had trimmed it that morning. Unlike many dark men it was not streaked with bristles redder or greyer than his hair.

Dean was busy with a couple who were inspecting a second-hand Jaguar. Roger approached a man who was deep in conversation with a younger replica of himself. Father and son. Son off to university. The car a reward for getting a place. It was that time of year, A level results had been published the previous Thursday. Roger got down to business.

Behind him was the newish Ford Jane Stevenson had hired for the weekend. He had checked it over, hoping to find an ear-ring or anything he could use as a genuine excuse for contacting her. There was nothing. No sweet wrappings, no ash. She was a remarkably tidy woman.

He could not forget her smile. It altered her sad but lovely face even if, as he suspected, it had been an effort for her to smile. He wondered what tragedy had caused the sadness and if he could be the one to make it go away.

On Sunday evening he had given up and gone home at six. He had been tired, it had been a long week. In the one-bedroomed flat he had once shared with Lily he had played music and sipped a large Scotch, realising that he ought to get out more as he had done when Lily was living with him. He rarely found the time to relax lately.

The following morning the car had been at the side of the showroom; the keys had been in the night-safe. Before he went home he looked up Jane's number in the telephone book. The address was correct but it was listed under G. Stevenson – from the days of her husband, he supposed. He had intended ringing her from home around seven, by which time, if she worked, she ought to be in. Soon after he got home himself his own phone rang.

'Your mother's been taken to hospital,' his father had said. 'I've been assured there's no cause for alarm, just some tests. But I knew you'd want to know.'

Roger spent the evening by his mother's bedside in the Hamilton Ward of Rickenham General. It was too late to speak to Jane by the time he got home.

The rain closed in and beat a tattoo on the roofs of the cars. The pungent smell of hot, wet tarmac filled the office. Roger closed up and went home.

On Tuesday night he was thwarted again. He tried Jane's number every half-hour but there was no reply. At ten thirty he gave up and went to bed.

9

Elaine Pritchard was exhausted. The rain had brought the customers in off the streets and Brockham's had been even busier than usual. On nights such as these she missed her husband. Not him so much, but someone else in the house when she got home. For two years she had been celibate, and one year ago she had become a statistic. One in three marriages ended in divorce; she was amongst that third. She was aware from articles she had read that when a couple lost a child the marriage did not get stronger through shared grief as might be supposed, but was frequently less likely to succeed. Not that Anna had been dead when Brian left, although she might as well have been. It had been the two years of shared nursing which had caused the strain. Brian had moved out but she would never allow herself to forget that he had always continued to do his share.

Ironically, the divorce came through the day before the funeral. Afterwards Elaine had gone back to office work but hated it because she was given a room on her own. She needed people around her, constant distraction, to stop her thinking of Anna and the break-up of her marriage. Seeing the advert for the job at Brockham's, she had applied for it and got it.

I'm lonely, she decided as she wandered through the sprawling bungalow where the three of them had once lived. She made tea and drank it in the kitchen, wondering what had happened to all their friends. Some had abandoned her when Brian left and the rest drifted away during and after Anna's illness as if tragedy was infectious. Not true friends then, she thought. But how could she blame them? There was nothing they could have done to diminish her grief or to dampen the rage she felt at the unfairness, the injustice and the revulsion which engulfed her. It was the latter that had driven Brian away.

And now Malcolm Graham was dead. At least he'd had sixty years of life, not fifteen followed by two when death would have been preferable.

She had got through the questions put to her by the police without letting her feelings for Graham show. She disliked the man and hated being anywhere near him, although she couldn't say why, but she had had to put up with it, he came with the job.

Tired as she was, Elaine knew she could not sit and think all night. Even though she lived within easy driving distance her sister was coming to stay. She would be arriving tomorrow and staying until the weekend. Elaine had welcomed the idea. It had come just at the right time.

Across the hall she stripped and showered, glad to be out of the navy cotton dress with its white collar and red and green dots that was Brockham's summer uniform. Feeling refreshed she made up the bed for Marion in Anna's old room. It had not been used since her death but it felt right now, somehow. The anniversary of Anna's death had just passed. Had Marion realised she would be arriving on the anniversary of the funeral? Yes, Marion would have known that and had decided to make sure Elaine was not on her own for it.

She would put some chicken pieces in the slow cooker overnight. They could be eaten cold with salad tomorrow evening. As she made her own meal, she thought back over the day. Jane Stevenson had come into the store but she was unsure if the woman had recognised her. Elaine was not surprised, it had been over a year since their last meeting at the hospital. Elaine had hesitated before speaking and by then it was too late. A customer had required her attention and Jane had gone to another counter for her purchase. When she looked up she was nowhere in sight. I hope she comes in again, she thought.

She had met Jane at the hospital when both Anna and Jane's husband had been waiting to see their respective specialists. Elaine recalled their first conversation well. The woman, roughly the same age as herself, seemed to be the one needing treatment. 'I know what it's like,' Elaine had said. 'It doesn't matter how much you love them, it can wear you down in the end.'

Jane had smiled. 'I slip across to the Coach and Horses after work, that's my bit of defiance, my way of coping,' she had said. Elaine remembered wishing she could do the same.

Their paths had crossed several more times then Anna had died and there was no further need for regular visits to Rickenham General.

She sat on the edge of the bed and thought of her mother who had done so much for Anna, for all of them, and who continued to do what she could for friends and family alike. Even on the day they had decided to celebrate her birthday she had spared a couple of hours for a neighbour in trouble. Saturday had not been the actual date of her birth but it was the only day on which they could all be together.

I'm so lucky to have her, she thought as tears filled her eyes. And Marion, who rings me every day. Few families were as close as theirs.

Ian had told Moira to expect him about eight but it was nearer to nine when he returned to Belmont Terrace and found his wife in the garden nursing a gin and tonic. It had stopped raining and the scent of flowers was overpowering. The soil was pitted where large drops of rain had hit it and the grass was still sodden. It had not deterred Moira from wiping a chair and sitting outside to admire her handiwork.

Ian had called in at the Crown and had one drink with Brenda, Short and Eddie but none of them was up to much when it came to conversation. The sight of that mutilated corpse was still with them. Brenda's divided loyalties had amused him. She was still trying to prove herself, to be one of the boys – which indeed she was – and drink with them after work, whilst half of her wanted to be at home with Andrew.

The light was beginning to fade; the evenings were growing shorter. In several weeks the end of summer would take them by surprise: they would wake to the first mist of autumn and start closing the windows at night. Ian was determined to enjoy what remained of the day. He poured himself a beer and sat in the garden chair next to his wife as insects flew around in the dusk. The only light came from the kitchen windows, four rectangles which threw their shadows on to the lawn.

Moira smiled but said nothing. She could smell the beer and recognised that expression, a mixture of tiredness, despair and anger. She had not spoken to him face to face since yesterday morning. He had been asleep when she got back from her night out and he had left without waking her that morning. As he was never a natural early riser, something was therefore seriously amiss. She had heard about Malcolm Graham but few details had been given via the media other than that the police were treating it as a suspicious death, a phrase which had now replaced the more thrilling word, murder. I've probably seen the man, I use Brockham's now and again, she thought. 'Have you eaten?'

Ian frowned. He had indigestion, he must have done at some point. Or were they hunger pangs he could feel?

'You don't know, do you? I'll get you something.' She stood up but Ian reached for her hand.

'No, not just yet. Stay here with me for a while.'

Moira sat down, her drink forgotten as she listened to the details of what had been found in that house in Spring Lane yesterday morning. 'Does it mean anything?' she asked, once the horrific facts had registered fully.

'Mean anything?'

'Well, is it ritualistic? Have there been other cases like it?'

'Ah, I see. I honestly don't know, Moira. But the thought had crossed our minds.' No local cases, he thought, certainly not around here, but she did have a point. However, Graham's home entertainment had been examined. Everything pointed to his having taken and processed the pictures himself, which precluded anyone other than the young women he had photographed being involved. In which case there would be no third party he might have threatened to reveal to the authorities, no one to whom he might have owed money had he bought the photos. And he had had plenty of money, this was another angle they were looking into.

'What about the people he worked with?' Moira was asking. 'Perhaps someone there hated him enough to do that.' She shuddered at the thought of the manner in which the man had been killed. No wonder Ian was quiet.

Ian shrugged and ran a hand through his hair. It needed trimming again. It was probably his imagination but it seemed to grow faster during the summer. 'So far he's a bit of an enigma. At work he kept a low profile, always around, always there if he was needed, but a sort of non-person.'

'But not at home, I bet. People like that always have another side to them.'

It was a statement. Moira had guessed that such a supposed nonentity would have something to hide. 'His wife couldn't stand him. She hasn't got an alibi, not for the time he was most likely killed, but she's not acting as if she needs one either.' He told her the rest, about the photographs and how some of the girls looked no more than fourteen or fifteen.

'Then he deserved to die,' Moira said flatly and unequivocally. 'Don't look at me like that, Ian. It's how I feel. Not saying it won't alter the fact.'

Brenda's instincts had suggested that a woman had killed Graham, and his ex-wife had said much the same thing. They were right, of that he was certain. What man would do that to another? What man would rob another of his maleness, even in death? Even hatred for one another would not necessarily remove the bond between men. A man would most often hit or injure the wife who had been unfaithful, not her lover, because he was a bloke, and blokes stick together even in those circumstances.

So, all they had to do was to find each and every one of the females who had been photographed then question them. The statements made by the women who worked at Brockham's would be double-checked but there was always the chance it had been a customer. It shouldn't take more than a year or so, he thought bitterly. And then all they had to do was to find the writer of those anonymous letters. They had been more bitter than his own thoughts, if that was possible. There had been three of them, adressed to no one, signed by no one, but hidden behind the false back of the wardrobe with the other things. Not destroyed, they had noticed, but not taken to the police either. 'You will die for what you have done,' one of them stated. Malcolm Graham had certainly died but was he killed by the author of those notes? Experts were going over them now. They had been written in large block capitals on cheap, lined paper. There were no envelopes to indicate whether they had been posted or delivered by hand, sent to Brockham's or his home address. The wavery block capitals suggested they had been written by a person using the opposite hand to the one they normally wrote with. These two things combined to make identification very difficult. Not my problem, Ian decided as his stomach gurgled.

'Who did you go for a drink with?'

'Scruffy Short and Brenda.'

'I wish you wouldn't do that, Ian. The Ugly Brute, Scruffy Short. Honestly.'

'Everyone calls him that. Wait until you meet him. A couple of uniforms came in. Sonia Saunders and someone else.'

'The one you call the Ice Maiden?'

'See? You're as bad as me. She wasn't so unbending tonight. She even managed a smile. She and her partner had a strange call on Friday. Some woman rang from the Coach and Horses to say her handbag had been stolen. Before she came off duty tonight they heard she'd got it back. The husband found it hanging on the back door knob. Nothing missing.'

'Nothing?' Ian shook his head. 'Someone with a conscience, maybe.'

'It still seems odd. Why risk going to the house with it? Anyway, it's another statistic towards the clear-up rate.' His stomach rumbled loudly again.

'Food.' Moira was on her feet. She picked up her glass and swallowed the contents. A pale moon, half formed, hung over the trees at the end of the garden. Soon it would be completely dark. She smiled as Ian reached for the newspaper, rolled it up and lashed out at a swarm of midges. Such a big man, she thought, and he's scared of a few tiny insects. For some reason he believed they would get in his hair or his mouth.

In the kitchen she pulled the window to against the moths and began to prepare a light supper.

10

Carmen slept badly on Monday night. At 7 a.m. on Tuesday she rang Sylvie Harris who sounded equally exhausted. 'If you're free this evening, why don't you come over for dinner?' she said. 'I think we'd better have a talk.'

'Thank you, I'd like that.'

'About half seven?' It would give her time to go home and change. Sylvie would not want to wear her store clothes to the house of her employer. It would be too positive a reminder of their respective positions.

By the late afternoon Carmen was tired. She regretted her invitation and hoped that her guest would not stay late. Sandy had been busy in the kitchen, there would be little for Carmen to do before they ate. The girl sensed something was wrong and did not attempt conversation, for which Carmen was grateful. She had spent the day in Rickenham Green and had returned in time to receive Neil's daily telephone call. She had never been so glad to hear his voice. They talked for twenty minutes. She had not wanted the call to end but for some reason she made no mention of Malcolm.

'Come in, I'm pleased you could make it,' Carmen said at precisely seven thirty when Sylvie arrived. 'Drink?' Her head ached and she wondered why the police had not come back to her. Surely they had searched the place by now. Even if they hadn't they would be curious as to why Malcolm's salary had been so generous. No, not generous; absurdly high. She caught her breath. There could be another explanation, Malcolm could have been lying to her all those years. At least Sylvie might be able to give her news of what had occurred at Brockham's that day.

'Just wine, thanks. The car, you know.'

Carmen poured two glasses and they sat down, neither woman quite sure how to broach the subject uppermost in both their minds.

'It's been a pig of a day.' Sylvie finally broke the silence. She reached for her bag before remembering that Carmen did not smoke. It would be a long evening, but worth it if she was finally able to take over from Malcolm.

'It's all right. Carry on,' Carmen told her, waving towards a large glass ashtray on a side table. 'How did it go with the police?'

'I think they managed to speak to quite a lot of people, although they're coming back again tomorrow. From what

75

I gather they just wanted to know who did or didn't like Malcolm and why, and, of course, what we were all doing over the weekend.' Sylvie shrugged. 'I didn't have an alibi.'

'Neither did I,' Carmen replied.

'What did you tell them?'

'Hardly anything. Malcolm worked for me, but, in retrospect, I realised I knew very little about him. We never socialised.' Not since I was a teenager, she thought. 'And you?'

'There wasn't anything much I could say.' Her face reddened. There was one thing, but it had no relevance.

Carmen reached over and touched the back of her hand. 'He told me, you know, about that one night.'

'Oh, God.' Sylvie looked down at the floor, more embarrassed by this revelation than she had been at the time.

'Did you tell the police?'

'No.'

'Then neither shall I. It was some time ago and it doesn't have any bearing on what happened to him. I know I oughtn't to say it, but Malcolm could be a very cruel and manipulative man. Good at his job, certainly, but not someone with whom to become involved. For your sake I'm glad it didn't go any further.

'Now I'll just see to the meal. I won't be a minute.'

Sylvie watched her leave the room. Carmen looked stunning. Cool, taupe-coloured trousers pleated at the waist, a cream blouse and gold sandals were set off by simple gold jewellery and nail polish. Her pale hair was tucked behind her ears. On Sylvie the outfit would have looked ridiculous, yet the older woman wore it with panache. The green linen dress Sylvie had changed into after work no longer seemed smart, merely dull.

Carmen returned, a wine bottle in her hand. 'We've time for one more, the food won't be long. Look,' she said as she refilled Sylvie's glass, 'there's something I want to ask you before we sit down.' She placed the bottle on the floor and reached down the side of the leather settee. In her hand were two envelopes; she held them out to Sylvie. 'Did you write these? No, don't answer. I can see by your face that you did. But why?'

'I hated him. He made a fool of me and the constant humiliation was too much to bear. I thought if you knew what he was like you'd get rid of him.'

Oh, I knew what he was like, she thought, and you don't know how I longed to get rid of him. 'Why not come to me? I'm not unapproachable, surely. Why stoop to this?'

'I didn't think you'd believe me. I thought if you thought someone else had written them you'd take more notice.'

'Well, it doesn't matter now.'

'If you knew they were from me why didn't you show them to the police? They're evidence, in a way.'

Carmen smiled. 'We girls must stick together. Besides, I know you're not capable of killing him. I realise why you did it. There were two reasons, the fact that you couldn't bear the constant reminder of what he did to you and, secondly, the fact that you wanted his job. I'm going to destroy them, Sylvie, it's the best thing to do. Come on, let's eat.' Just look at me now, she thought. From victim to law-breaker overnight. 'Anyway, let's hope Malcolm destroyed the ones you sent him. That's what made me believe you'd written to me.'

'What?' Sylvie's mouth dropped open and she clutched at the back of the dining-room chair.

'Did you think he wouldn't tell me?'

'But I didn't, Carmen. I never wrote to Malcolm.'

Carmen pulled out her own chair and sat down. Sylvie did the same. 'Well, somebody did,' she said with a frown. What the hell was going on? She knew Sylvie well enough to judge that she was telling the truth. If she hadn't written those threatening letters, who had? Had Malcolm destroyed them or had the police found them?

Knowing that Carmen had destroyed the letters and would not bring up the subject of her single night with Malcolm, Sylvie slept well. On Wednesday morning she arrived at work ready to face the day. She felt no sorrow at Malcolm's fate, and she had no reason to think the police would consider her to be a suspect.

With a smile to encourage the rest of the staff she went about the daily business of the store and made an effort to be pleasant to the police when they arrived and, later, when they asked to speak to her again.

'God, they're wanting to know where we all were over the

weekend,' one of the girls told her. 'They must think someone here killed him.'

Sylvie's smile did not falter. 'Of course they don't. They're just doing their job.' She was not concerned that her movements had already been questioned the previous day; she understood that those who had been closest to Malcolm were the most likely suspects and she had worked with him for many years. But when she walked into the staff room she was surprised to see it was the same pair of officers who were waiting to speak to her.

'We're not entirely satisfied with some of the answers we've been receiving regarding Mr Graham,' Inspector Short began.

'Oh? In what way?'

'Well, for instance, how come, after so many years, not one person here claims to know anything about him? You worked closely with him, Mrs Harris, you probably knew him better than anyone else here and you were the one who alerted us at a very early stage. What is it that is not being said?'

She glanced at DC Gibbons, who appeared not to be listening as she picked at a fingernail. 'I don't think there was much to know. He told me he lived alone. His interests were solitary, gardening, that sort of thing. Any friends he had were in Frampton or at the Elms. He didn't mix with work colleagues.'

'All very bland. But?'

Sylvie Harris felt the tell-tale flush rise up from her neck and knew that it was time for an admission. 'All right. If you must know he was a lecher. Always after anything in a skirt, not that it got him far.'

'I see. He tried it on with you, did he?'

'Yes. And I told him what he could do.'

'Visit you at home, did he?'

'No.' Her face had probably given her away. They can check, she realised. She had no real knowledge of the way in which the law worked but they might have some sort of warrant, someone might be at her house as they spoke, taking fingerprints. 'I'm mistaken. He did come once. I'd left something at work one evening. He brought it home for me.' The bedroom, there might be fingerprints in the bedroom. What had he touched, beside her, in his cold, brutal manner?

'Just the once?'

'Yes.'

'Complaints, were there? From other female staff?'

'No.'

'Then you were the only recipient of his advances. Does that make him a lecher? Surely it's the opposite. You ought to have been flattered.'

Sylvie said nothing. She couldn't without making it worse for herself.

'Or could it be that it was the other way around, that he rebuffed you?'

'How dare you suggest such a thing?'

'I dare because I am a police officer, Mrs Harris, and a man has been brutally murdered and we need to know why and by whom.'

'It's no more than he deserved, he was brutal himself.' The words were out of her mouth before she could stop them. She hated this untidy, odious little man and his insinuations. God, she would have to be more careful.

'I think,' John Short said with a smile, 'we had better start again. But first, perhaps you'd like to give us a more detailed account of your movements over the whole of last weekend, starting from Friday night.' John Short was bored. He hated interviewing suspects, he hated interviewing anyone. Why wasn't Roper here? It was right up his street. Because Roper was arranging for someone to get into the word processor and organising the interviews of the six people who had been at the Talbots' house on Saturday night. And there were all those photographs to go through, with little chance of discovering who they were of. He, John, could be of more use reading the reports. For some reason he sensed more from the written word than he did from people. Still, he had caught this woman out in a lie, perhaps he could do so again. And, if she wasn't lying, she had provided a fraction more evidence that the crime was sexually motivated. Yet somehow, despite her air of vindictiveness, he could not picture Mrs Harris mutilating the body in such a manner. She was too fastidious. If she wanted someone dead she would slip them an overdose or cut their brake cables. It would be impersonal, she would not use a knife.

Elaine Pritchard was the last of the staff to be seen again, and only then because Brenda had felt her dislike of Graham went deeper than she was prepared to reveal. She gave a precise and checkable account of her movements; shopping on Saturday morning, her first Saturday off for three weeks – she could provide Switch card receipts which were dated – then a trip to Ipswich to see her mother.

'I stayed the night,' she said, blushing becomingly. Short resisted the urge to lean forward and kiss her full lips. 'It was her birthday, you see, and we had a bit too much to drink. I didn't dare risk driving back.' But it had all gone wrong. Her sister had arrived late, her mother later still. And they believe I haven't guessed, she thought. They're both trying to protect me.

'Very sensible,' Short said, ignoring Brenda who raised her eyebrows in disgust as his obvious attempt at flirting.

'It's no one here,' Short said, tugging at his moustache, a habit which irritated Brenda. 'That Harris woman had it in for him, frustrated, that's her trouble, but nothing that a large portion wouldn't cure. She might even have written those threatening letters but can you see her doing him in like that?'

A large portion, my God, does anyone still use that phrase? Brenda thought. But she had to agree with his sentiments. She shook her head. 'No. She might be capable of murder, but not that way. And she didn't strike me as being clever enough to get away with it, she wasn't even able to stop herself blurting out the truth about Graham's visit to her house – where, I'm sure you'll agree, a little more than the returning of a forgotten package took place.' She sighed. 'Besides, none of the fingerprints match.' There had been few in Graham's place other than his own, yet someone had gained entry and had gone up or had been taken up to his bedroom. Someone who had known what would happen there and had been careful not to touch anything.

Short nodded dolefully. 'It's after twelve, we might as well get back,' he said.

Brenda had twenty minutes in which to eat a sandwich and drink a mug of coffee before she was on her way out of the station again. The Chief had asked her to accompany him.

John Greville had been the manager at the Elms Golf and Country Club for fifteen years. His physical appearance had changed during that time but his obsequious manner remained the same. And he liked to keep on the right side of the police, especially as John Cotton, head of the scene-of-crime department, put in an occasional appearance, as did DCI Roper and his good friend, James Harris, the police surgeon who was actually a member. And one of their members had been murdered. The talk had been of nothing else since they had heard the news.

'Ah, Inspector Roper, we meet again. Come through to my office and I'll arrange for some coffee.'

Ian raised his eyebrows at Brenda behind the man's back as they followed him through the foyer to a well-appointed room behind the reception area. There were comfortable chairs and cared-for pot plants as well as the accoutrements of a busy modern office.

The club was about three miles from the centre of Rickenham Green and had a waiting list. Apart from golf there was the bar and a billiard room, and private functions were catered for. More recently had come the addition of a gym and sauna. Membership fees were extortionate but enough people found the money to pay them. Part of a legacy had enabled Doc Harris to join, more for the malt whisky than the golf, and occasionally Ian or John Cotton were signed in as his guests.

'What can you tell us about Malcolm Graham?' Ian asked, aware that no explanation for their visit was necessary.

'I didn't like him.'

Ian was taken aback. After all the waffle they'd heard here was the first, and the least expected, source to come out with such an unambiguous statement. 'Why not?'

Greville actually took a few seconds to consider his answer. 'There was something underhand about him. He would eavesdrop on conversations without appearing to.' He coughed, one pudgy hand to his mouth. 'And, well, you might think me a prude, but some of the remarks he addressed to the male members were downright crude.'

Someone had said he wasn't the marrying type, that he was set in his ways, but Ian couldn't remember who because it was not someone he had spoken to himself. But he had been married and his wife had complained about his sexual habits. Was Greville trying to say the man was gay? 'Could you be more exact?'

'I'm not prepared to repeat the sort of things he said, but they concerned female members, comments about certain parts of their anatomy, and what he would like to do to them, that kind of thing.'

'Locker-room talk?'

'Yes, maybe, but more crude and not confined to the locker-rooms.'

'Did anyone comment about this to you? Male or female?'

'No. I picked it up for myself. The people who come here don't like to make waves. If anyone found what he said offensive they tended to move away or ignore him.'

So the killer could be a jealous man, Ian thought, maybe one who had overheard more than he was meant to, one who believed Malcolm Graham had actually done to his wife what Graham had only said he wished to do. 'Mr Greville, do you think you can remember the people he talked of in such a manner?'

'Yes, quite easily. I . . . well, it sounds a bit off if I say there are only a handful of really attractive female members, I mean, I wouldn't want to be accused of sexism, but they were the ones who caught his eye. Especially the younger ones.'

'Younger?' Ian was aware of Brenda's interest, aware that something had just occurred to her. It would have to wait.

'We have a junior section. It was started to bring on young golfers, between the ages of twelve and sixteen. Only two girls showed any interest but unfortunately the one who looked the most promising gave up. Malcolm used to talk to her. I could see she didn't like it at first, he'd whisper things. Then as soon as I decided I ought to say something to her father her attitude changed. She seemed prepared to put up with his company now and again, then she disappeared.'

'Disappeared?'

'Oh, I don't mean literally. She stopped coming here a couple of years ago. Her father's a member. He said she plays on the public greens now.'

'We'll need her name, Mr Greville. How old would she be now?'

Greville frowned. 'Seventeen, I imagine. Why?'

'Good. We can talk to her without involving her parents if necessary.'

'That's a relief. It wouldn't look well for the club if there was something not quite right going on.'

'I would have thought having one of your members murdered was hardly within the bounds of what was quite right.'

Greville got up without answering and got the girl's name and address from a list on the computer. Ian thanked him and they left.

'You don't want to question the members?' Brenda asked as their feet scattered the gravel of the car-park at the side of the building.

'It might not be necessary. We'll see what Caroline Innes has to say first.'

They got into the car. Ian had parked under a tree, one of the elms from which the club had acquired its name, and left the windows open but it was still stuffy. The heatwave had returned but less ferociously than before. 'We've got three versions,' he said, 'a conscientious and loyal employee, although hardly known by the staff, a saint in Frampton and some sort of Lothario here at the club.'

'Not forgetting how his ex-wife described him. What next? The girl?'

'Yes. The girl. Get in touch with Alan Campbell, will you? See if anything's turned up out at Frampton and if he's managed to break into that damn machine.' Ian had decided to let Alan go ahead. He was the best man for the job and only words would be displayed on the screen, not visual images. Names, hopefully, and addresses if they were very lucky.

Ian swung out of the drive. There was little traffic on the B road which led to the coast. Anyone with any sense and who did not have to work would be on the beach already or enjoying the privacy of their garden. He wished he could join them. Sweat stood out on his brow and his shirt stuck to his spine. And Brenda Gibbons looked as cool and unruffled as ever. One day he might ask her how she did it.

Alan's voice crackled over the communications system. 'Frampton have one sighting for that night, sir, but it mightn't mean anything A car was seen parked in a gateway about ten past eight on Saturday night and was still there at eight fifteen,' he said in answer to Brenda's question. 'A bloke walking down to the pub noticed it. He lives in a cottage nearby and swears it wasn't there when he looked out of his bedroom window earlier in the evening. Anyway, he's a farmer, a regular at the pub. He leaves home at the same time every evening, walks down to the village, has two pints then walks back again.'

'Anyone in the car? Courting couple, maybe, someone reading a map?'

'No, it was empty. He was certain of that.'

'Make? Registration mark?' Brenda knew the answer before it was given. There was no reason for the farmer to have noted either.

'He didn't notice. A dark blue car, that's all he remembers. He went home at nine thirty as usual but the car wasn't there then.

'A motorist also came forward to say she saw it as she was driving home from a friend's house. She knew it was eight fifteen because she'd just looked at her watch knowing she was late. They've faxed through the two statements from Frampton and a map to show the proximity of the car to Graham's house. It would be easy to reach it over the field at the back.'

'And the word processor?'

Alan laughed, surprising Brenda. 'You're going to love this. It's all gardening data. I've checked, it isn't some kind of code, the numbers on the disks represent the months of the year.'

'Oh, wonderful! Thanks, Alan. Did you get all that?' she asked Ian who was tapping his fingers on the wheel because they were stuck behind a tractor towing a trailer full of straw. Wisps escaped and landed on the bonnet before falling to the ground.

'I did. Bloody thing, why can't it pull over for us?'

'Probably because there's nowhere for him to do so.'

Ian grunted. He was not in the mood for female logic.

11

Caroline Innes lived with her parents in a detached cottage amidst farmland and woods. The natural beauty of the 150-year-old property had been ruined by the addition of carriage lamps, leaded windows and an excess of garden ornaments. These additions may not have been to Ian's taste but he recognised it had taken money to have them put in place.

At two thirty on a hot August afternoon sunlight bathed the front of the building. All the visible windows were open, as was the sturdy wooden front door. Raised voices could be heard from within as Ian and Brenda got out of the car. The argument was too heated for their arrival to have been noticed.

They walked up the narrow path towards the house, resisting the temptation to stop and listen to what was being said. Ian reached for the brass knocker and let it fall with a thud. This sound was followed by a sudden silence.

'Yes?' A man almost as tall as Ian appeared in the doorway. Although probably still in his thirties he wore grey flannel trousers and a white shirt with a paisley cravat. He might have stepped straight out of the 1920s into the year 2000. All that was missing was a tennis racquet because he was already holding a tumbler of gin and tonic.

'We'd like to speak to Caroline,' Ian said, having introduced himself and Brenda. 'I take it you're her father?'

'Stepfather. Norman Michaels.' Michaels seemed unsure whether he was expected to shake hands. He half raised the empty one then dropped it. 'I married Caro's mother ten years ago. I've brought that girl up as though she was my own.' He shook his head. 'I can tell you, there's no reward in doing your duty. Is she in trouble?' he asked belatedly, still seemingly more upset by the row than the reason for their visit. But his concern for his daughter seemed genuine. He sighed. 'She's going through an awkward stage but she's a good girl generally. I can't believe she's done anything illegal.'

Ian would have liked to ask what the current problem was, but perhaps it was no more than the usual turmoil of a house containing an adolescent not quite past the stage of rebellion. 'We'd just like to ask her a few questions. She isn't in trouble as far as we know but we think she might be able to help us. Is she here?' It might have been the wife he was arguing with, and not Carolline's raised voice they had heard.

'She's here all right, but I don't know for how much longer. You'd better come in.'

They were shown into a lounge which stretched the length of

the building and which had obviously once been two rooms. The inside was far more tasteful than the outside had led them to believe it would be, so maybe those added fixtures were the legacy of a previous occupant. 'I'll get her,' Michaels said. 'She's sulking in the kitchen.'

Caroline Innes appeared a few seconds later. She was a pretty girl with long fair hair and a neat figure. Her face was red and the stiff way in which she moved showed that she was angry. Both Ian and Brenda saw at once that this was one of Malcolm Graham's models. There was a photograph of her in their possession, taken, Ian guessed, a couple of years ago.

'I'll leave you to it,' Michaels said when he had told the girl that the police wanted to question her. 'I hope you have better luck than me. I'll be outside if you need me.'

After the few seconds of silence which followed his departure they heard the chink of bottle and glass then a door closing somewhere at the back of the house.

Caroline sat down. She was limp now, as if she had expended all her energy upon arguing with her stepfather.

Ian nodded at Brenda. The girl might feel antagonistic towards men just then, a woman's touch might be better.

'Caroline, did you know a man called Malcolm Graham?'

'Yes. He was a member at the Elms. I heard he was murdered.'

'And how did you feel about that?'

She glanced up, defiance in her face. 'How should I have felt? I didn't know him. An old man like that was of no interest to me.'

'I see. Why did you stop playing golf at the Elms?' Brenda perched on the edge of an armchair. The girl was hostile and it was a less intimidating position than standing over her. Ian remained on his feet but out of the girl's peripheral vision.

'I prefer the public course.'

'Caroline,' Brenda began gently, 'there's no point in lying. We have a photograph of you, it's no more than two years old, one which was taken by Mr Graham.'

'A photograph? Oh, my God. So that's what it was.' She slumped forward, her head in her hands and did not speak until the shock had worn off. Swallowing hard she asked, 'Will my parents need to know?'

'Not necessarily, not if you tell us the truth. Was this anything to do with your argument earlier?'

She nodded. 'Yes. In a way. Mum's out, she goes to pottery class on Wednesday afternoons during the holidays. I thought it would be easier to break the news to Dad first. I told him I wanted to leave home within the next few days. As soon as I heard that man was dead I was terrified I'd be found out. You see, I was convinced he didn't touch me but there had to be a reason he wanted me undressed. It would kill my parents if they knew. It was only the once, I swear to God, and I didn't really know what was happening until it was too late. Mum's always said she doesn't want me to leave home but I thought Dad might soften her up a bit. He refused to. He feels the same way as she does, he says eighteen is soon enough to live on my own.'

'You get on well with your stepfather?'

'Yes. I hardly remember my real father. Norman's always been good to me and he and Mum love each other even though he's five years younger than her.'

It sounded to Brenda as though Caroline Innes believed love between an older woman and a younger man was totally impossible. 'Look, I don't know what you'll tell them about the reason for us wanting to speak to you, but would you be prepared to come into Rickenham and tell us the whole story? It'll be easier there.'

'Yes. Yes, I would. Right now?' She seemed relieved to have been given the chance to talk about it.

'If you can.'

'Okay. I'll just let Dad know. I can get the bus home.'

'No. We'll arrange transport.'

Caroline was silent throughout the short journey. Neither Brenda nor Ian knew what excuse she had given Michaels and they decided it was better not to know.

An hour later they realised the sort of man Graham had been and why someone had hated him enough to have killed him in such a way. But that someone wasn't Caroline or her parents. They had been on holiday in France until Monday. 'They insisted I went,' she had told them. 'Dad said it might be the last holiday we had together, that I probably wouldn't want to know them once I go away to college.'

Jennifer Michaels was an infant school teacher, Norman a

celebrated artist (even if they had not heard of him) and their daughter was still at school. All three names went into the computer anyway, despite the fact that the ferry company with whom they had sailed had confirmed all three passengers were on board for both journeys.

Neil Longman had been out of the country for a week and had no idea that Malcolm Graham was dead. There had been many women in his life but he, like Carmen, had never married. Now he believed he had found someone who understood him and his needs, someone who shared his views. Even if they married, an idea which appealed more and more, theirs would not be a conventional marriage. They both needed space, they might even keep their individual properties. He would certainly have to retain his flat in London. By the time he returned to Rickenham Green he had made up his mind to propose to her.

Carmen was expecting him. They were going out to dinner, to a newly opened restaurant in Saxborough, after which they were staying overnight in a nearby hotel so neither of them would have to drive.

She stood in the doorway, a silver clutch bag in her hand, ready to go out. Her dress was a shift which shimmered as she moved, changing colour with the light: sometimes grey, sometimes green, sometimes blue. It was simple, elegant and expensive. In her ears were the pearl and gold earrings Neil had given her for Christmas just after they had met.

Neil kissed her and pulled her to him, frowning when he felt a slight resistance. 'Don't I get a welcome home drink before we leave?'

'We'll be late.'

He helped her into the car and started the engine, wondering why his reception had been a little on the cool side. Had she changed her mind about him during his absence? He had telephoned most days and she'd seemed pleased to hear from him. And they were in plenty of time.

It was several miles later before he asked what was wrong. He knew with certainty that he didn't want to lose her. 'Is it something I've done, or not done?'

'Of course not, Neil. It's just we've had problems at the store . . .'

'Murdered?' he said, once Carmen had explained.

'Yes. And it's made everybody edgy, including myself. We're all suspects, you see.'

Neil laughed loudly. 'Oh, honestly. No one could picture you as a murderer, Carmen. The police have to ask a lot of questions, and you were his employer after all, you probably knew him better than anyone.'

'I know.'

He reached across and stroked her thigh, the material of her dress sliding against its underslip. 'Don't worry, darling. It'll all get sorted out in the end.'

Carmen glanced at him, at his handsome profile and short cropped hair the colour of her own, although his was naturally fair, and knew that they made a perfect pair, that at long last, she had found a man with whom she wanted to share her life. And if it all came out, she would lose him. She bit her lip, thinking it would have been better if she had never met him.

'It can't affect us, please don't think that,' Neil said, as if he had read her mind. 'It's been a shock for you. Do you want to talk about it?'

'No, I don't. I think I'm sick and tired of talking about it.'

'Then you'd better cheer up and enjoy the evening whilst we've got the chance.'

'What do you mean?' Carmen stifled the note of rising panic quickly. Was he going to leave her anyway?

'I meant before they handcuff you and throw you into a cell. Just a joke,' he added quickly, remembering that Malcolm had been with her for over twenty years and that she would be feeling the loss. He had met the man once and had disliked him on sight although he had no idea why this should be as he normally took time to form an opinion.

They were already on the outskirts of Saxborough. Carmen decided to ask the question and get it over with rather than wait until they were eating. 'Neil, what would you do if you found out there was something shady in my past?'

'Shady? You are in a strange mood tonight. Carmen, people like you just don't have shady pasts. I do wish you'd stop worrying so much.'

'But supposing there was something – what about your career? You know what the press are like these days, they love to dig the dirt on any MP. I mean, it wouldn't be you who'd done anything, they couldn't ask for your resignation, but it might mean your parliamentary career came to a standstill.'

Neil swung into the restaurant car-park and turned off the ignition. 'If there's something you want to tell me, tell me now, Carmen. Get it off your chest, as they say. I think you're in a state because of what's happened, but let's be straight with one another, that's all I've ever wanted from the woman I love.'

The woman I love . . . Carmen knew he meant it. She could not risk losing him yet. In the end she might do so, but for as long as she could get away with it she would remain silent. She leaned over and kissed his cheek. 'You're right. I'm a bit over-wrought. There isn't anything I want to say.' She smiled. 'Now let's see if this food is as marvellous as that colour supplement would have us believe.'

She held his arm as they crossed the car-park, more to steady herself than out of the genuine affection she felt for him. Enjoy it while it lasts, she thought as tears started to prickle behind her eyelids.

'Bring her in,' Ian said, his stomach tightening with excitement.

Inspector Short had been more than efficient. British Telecom had not yet had enough time to compile a list of Graham's calls but they had come back to them with one number. On the day the body was discovered Short had dialled 1471 and made a note of the number and the time he had received his last call. What they didn't know was whether or not he had answered the phone. However, as it was timed at 19.06 it seemed likely he had as the Talbots had confirmed he was still alive after that time. The call had been made from a public telephone box in Saxborough. BT had supplied its location.

'Canadian Avenue is only three or four streets away from where Diane Hicks lives,' Short had added.

Yes, it was possible for resentment to build up over a period of years, Ian thought. And maybe she had lied when she said she had no idea where he was working, maybe she was broke and had somehow heard how much he was earning, a point they had yet to take up with Carmen Brockham.

It was five thirty on Wednesday evening, the time when most people were packing up and going home for the evening. Not Ian, though, not that night. Not for him the joys of the garden and some conversation with Moira that did not involve crime. She's going round to Deirdre's anyway, he recalled. I wouldn't see her if I did go home.

By lunchtime that day they had learned that there was a will, one made in the early days when Malcolm and Diane had lived together. In the days when he had nothing to leave he had made his wife the sole beneficiary. There had been no children then.

'Is there a will?' Diane Hicks had asked. Strange that she had not known of its existence. But she could have meant, is there still a will in my favour? And what of the daughters? Was it worth questioning them? It was not unheard of for victims of incest or violence to kill the parent responsible. No, we'll talk to Diane first, he decided.

'Sir?' Eddie Roberts interrupted his line of thought. 'Unless he went to another solicitor to update the will this one still stands. The man I spoke to, Peter Harcourt, thinks it's unlikely there's another one as Graham has continued to use the firm for various bits and pieces over the years.'

'Such as?' Ian turned to face the room where shadows slanted across the hard-wearing cord carpet.

'Nothing of interest to us. A motoring accident two years ago. Someone hit his stationary car at traffic lights. Three years prior to that he wanted advice over a possible neighbour dispute.'

'Possible?' Surely old John Talbot and his wife hadn't gone round there with a knife because he'd threatened to sue them?

'Jack and Elizabeth Porter, number two Spring Lane. They had some out of control shrubs up against the boundary fence for which Graham was responsible. He kept on having to repair it. Harcourt suggested the best way round it was to talk to them tactfully, they might not have realised just how bad the problem was. Turned out to be the case. Matter resolved. Before that they did the conveyancing on the house in Frampton, and some years earlier, the will. And, knowing Graham, if there had been another will, a copy would have been amongst all that paperwork.'

'Thanks, good work. Gives us someone with a motive, no matter how thin.'

'Where's Inspector Short?'

Ian smiled. Eddie Roberts was always respectful and would not dream of calling the man Scruffy either to his face or behind his back, and especially not in front of the Chief Inspector. 'Gone to pick up Diane Hicks.' Could it be that simple? Not sex, but money, the crime disguised to make it seem other motives were involved? No, it was unlikely now that they had Caroline Innes's statement.

'No good, sir.' Brenda came through the open door of the general office and sat at her desk. She kicked off her low-heeled sandals and rubbed her heels. 'All the Talbots' guests agree with what they told us. They were all too engrossed in their cards to have noticed anything. Two of the couples left at eleven thirty, the third nearer midnight. None of them remembered seeing a car in the gateway, but they weren't really looking and, as far as we know, it wasn't there by then. And, I suspect, one couple at least had had more to drink than was wise.'

'No luck there, then,' Ian said. 'We're waiting upon Miss Diane Hicks, or Mrs Malcolm Graham, whatever she chooses to call herself. She'll be in for a shock if she doesn't know her husband's situation.'

'A shock, or a pleasant surprise,' Brenda said with a grin. 'Do you need me or can I push off?'

'Go home. Go and enjoy your house and the sea. Don't worry about us slaving away in this greenhouse.'

'Thanks, sir. I won't. Goodnight.'

While he waited for John Short to come back he reconsidered his opinion of Brenda. He had turned down her application for promotion some time ago. She would have had no trouble getting through the separate parts of the exams but her attitude hadn't been right and she had not gained sufficient experience. Andrew Osborne was doing her good. If she reapplied he would propose her.

'I'm bloody sick of late nights,' John Short said as he slumped over his desk. He hadn't seen Nancy for almost a week and he couldn't wait to get between her silk sheets and enjoy the musty smell of her and the plumpness of her body. It was an ideal arrangement, no strings attached. He did not ask because he did not want to know what she did on the nights when she was not with him. The reverse was also true. Scruffy Short loved women and he made a pass at almost any that came his way. But because of his appearance and a total lack of tact his advances were almost always rejected. He never took offence, there were always more on the horizon.

'So are we all,' Ian replied, 'but until we start getting some definite leads we're all in the same boat.' Damn, he thought, catching Alan Campbell's eye and seeing him smile. Another cliché. 'Let's just piece together what we've learned today then I, for one, shall retire to the pub.'

It was Inspector Short who summarised. 'We know Graham was into pornography and that it is very unlikely anyone else was involved. We've got his equipment and the results of his amateur efforts. He preferred young girls, but so do a lot of men. Sorry, sir. We have the photographs of them and we've spoken to one of them. His ex-wife describes him as a pig and the women he worked with didn't like him, a fact they weren't able to disguise, despite what they said.

'Carmen Brockham didn't like him either. In fact, I got the impression she was pleased he was dead.

'Apart from work there doesn't seem to be anyone else in his life. No real friends in Frampton and none at the Elms. So that narrows the killer down to colleagues at Brockham's or someone who hasn't come into the frame yet. Or one of the females in his collection.' Short sighed. The field was still wide open.

The photographs had been examined in detail. Many of them had been taken years before and experts were computer-enhancing them to age the girls to see if any of them was recognisable as a woman, hopefully a woman with whom they had already come into contact.

'We also have Caroline Innes's statement to back up the sexual side.'

Ian, leaning against the windowsill with his arms folded, nodded. Graham had been a revolting man if what she had told them was true. He had met Caroline at the Elms when she was fifteen. One evening when her parents were elsewhere she had sprained an ankle when her ball went into the rough. He had offered her a lift home then said he needed to call in at his house to collect something. He had invited her in.

'I must've been stupid,' she had told Ian. 'I mean, he was an old man, someone who knew my parents, I had no reason not to trust him. He gave me a brandy, he said it would ease the pain. My ankle was really throbbing by then. He strapped it up for me. By then I was half asleep. I'm sure he must've put something in the drink because he didn't pour out much. Mum and Dad always let me have a sip of something at Christmas and the odd glass of wine so it wasn't as if I'd never tasted alcohol. The next thing I remember was that he was dressing me. He looked shocked, as if he hadn't expected me to come around so quickly. He made me drink black coffee, three mugs of it, then he gave me a hundred pounds not to tell anyone.

'I wasn't totally sure what had happened, but he didn't have sex with me, I knew that much. I thought about going to the police, but who would've believed me? I wasn't hurt or raped, there was no evidence, and if they'd taken a drink or drugs test they'd have decided I was making it up, trying to cause trouble. Besides, even if I was believed, he'd deny it or say I was willing.'

'But you were under age,' Ian had told her.

'I know. But I was also scared and ashamed. All the time I believed it must have somehow been my fault.'

It appeared that once he had taken the photographs he had no more use for her. There had been no request for a repetition, no mention of it, nothing. Caroline had left the Elms anyway. She had not been able to endure the sight of him. She had also said she did not know of anyone else who might have had the same unfortunate experience.

'The question is,' Short continued, 'was it the same with all of the girls or were some of them willing, especially if he offered them money?'

'But where did the money come from? Have we found out yet?' Brenda asked.

'Alan Campbell has a theory but it will be hard to prove. We know what Graham's salary was, and it was more than generous, but Alan believes he photographed these girls then, when they were older, settled, married, whatever, he blackmailed them, threatening to expose them if they didn't pay up. Then part of that money was used to pay off the next lot of young girls. Caroline Innes is still at school. He couldn't get at her without exposing himself, but he might have been waiting until she applied for a job and then he'd threaten to send the pictures to her future employers if she didn't pay up.'

'And one of these girls murdered him, turned the tables, if you like,' Ian suggested. There had been alcohol in Graham's system and traces of barbiturates, not enough to knock him out but enough to slow him down, to inhibit his reaction time.

'I agree that it points more to one of the girls than the staff at Brockham's,' Eddie Roberts added. 'Especially as none of the pictures match any of the staff there.'

'Not necessarily.' Alan Campbell stood up and stretched. He was starving. He was always starving even though he ate plenty and often. But he still appeared undernourished. 'People change. Once those pictures have been computer-enhanced we might find a similarity.'

'Time to go home,' Ian said. 'Who's going to join me in the Crown?'

John Short hesitated. 'Yeah. I'll come with you.' Nancy might be out or entertaining at home. He hadn't had a chance to ring her. Better to try later when the coast would be clear.

Eddie Roberts shook his head. 'No, I'm off home before the wife forgets who I am.'

'Alan?'

'No, thanks, sir. It's an Indian take-away for me.'

Out in the street Ian loosened his tie. A pint would be welcome, it was a shame the company was not. But to his surprise Scruffy Short had the landlord and his wife laughing in no time. He felt a bit put out. This was his pub, Bob and Connie were his friends. Short ought not to be the centre of attention, he thought sulkily.

A second surprise awaited him at home. Moira was in the kitchen, sitting at the table. She wore a pink striped summer dress with no bra, and strappy sandals. Her face was flushed, her eyes over-bright 'Got a taxi,' she said with a giggle as she reached unsteadily for the glass of wine she had managed to pour without spilling.

'Moira?' This was normally his role. Far too often he had returned home in such a state. For Moira it was unheard of.

What was happening? He was being usurped all over the place.

'Had a bloody good night with Deirdre,' she said as she got to her feet and headed for the kitchen door unsteadily.

Feeling virtuous, Ian made tea and drank it standing up, gazing out at what could be seen of the garden by the kitchen light. So much for adding a touch of my wife's common sense to the case, he thought before joining her in bed where she was already sound asleep.

12

There had been no other woman in the two years since Lily packed her bags and went back home. Roger Pender had known she was married but she had lived apart from her husband for almost a year when they first met. How well she had hidden the fact that she still loved him, how quickly she had jumped at the chance when he had asked her back. And now that she was safely in the past, the hurt and sleepless nights forgotten, he was free to think about Jane Stevenson. A little out of practice, he was not sure what he would say to her or even if she would want to see him. Circumstances had prevented him contacting her on Monday night, on Tuesday there had been no answer. Now he had been reassured that his mother's condition was not serious there was nothing to stop him ringing again today. He admitted part of his hesitation was due to the fear of a repeat of the situation he had found himself in with Lily. I might have got it all wrong, anyway, he decided. Jane Stevenson had hired a car and told him she was visiting her mother; she wore no wedding ring but that did not preclude her taking a husband or boyfriend with her. 'Tonight,' he said as he tidied his desk. 'I'll try again this evening.' Surely she wouldn't be out two nights in a row.

Yesterday's heavy showers had provided only a temporary relief from the heat. Once more a haze shimmered over the tarmac and the top of the soil in the raised borders that divided the forecourt from the pavement was dry and crumbly again even if the plants did look a little fresher.

Dean was in the office and it was too early for customers. He opened up at nine but it was rare anyone came in before ten.

With his hands in his jacket pockets he strolled around the used cars, checking they were all clean and their prices displayed clearly. Reaching the car Jane had hired he opened the door and sat behind the steering wheel. It had been through the car-wash at the back of the premises sometime on Monday morning, like every returned car. Each vehicle was unlocked as soon as Roger arrived for work. It would look unprofessional to fumble around for keys if a customer was interested in one of them.

Why am I so insecure? he wondered. It's obvious she'd like to see me again, she was almost flirting with me when she came in. Well, ring her tonight then you'll know one way or another, common sense told him. If she was married or not interested, she'd tell him. He glanced at the dashboard, frowning; something was puzzling him, but he couldn't think what.

'Coffee's up,' Dean called from the door of the showroom.

Grateful for the distraction and knowing he would have to listen to Dean's latest exploits as far as girls were concerned, he sauntered back across the forecourt with a smile on his face. He might be almost twenty years older but he felt in much the same position as Dean.

Two cars were sold that day, an optimistic omen. Wandering around his flat with a beer in his hand, Roger waited until precisely seven o'clock before picking up the telephone. Enough time for Jane to have returned from work and had a cup of tea, or whatever other ritual made up that part of her day. He was staring out over the corrugated roofs of the row of garages which belonged to the flats when, after nine rings, someone finally answered his call. He had just talked himself into thinking Jane worked nights. 'Hello, is that Jane Stevenson?'

'Yes, it is.'

Her voice sounded different, not as soft and certainly not as confident as when he had spoken to her face to face. 'This is Roger Pender, of Pender's Garage. I just . . . well, I wondered . . . Oh, God, I must sound like an idiot, I'll start again. I'd like to take you out to dinner one night. May I?' She did not answer. In the background he heard a man's voice. 'Who is it, love?' or words to that effect. Roger's disappointment was acute. Her answer would obviously be no. And he may well have caused trouble for her. 'Hello? Are you still there?'

'Yes. I'm sorry, but I think you've got the wrong number. Or the wrong Jane Stevenson. I know Pender's Garage, I pass it every day, but I've never met you. I don't know who you are, I'm afraid.'

He had caused trouble. She was being cagey. Jane's bloke could not be aware she had hired a car. 'No, it's I who should apologise. When you came into the showroom I knew that I wanted to see you again. I had to ring you. I didn't know you were involved with anyone. I'll let you go now. I hope everything went all right with your mother. Goodbye, Jane.'

'Mr Pender, wait. Hold on a minute. I don't understand. You know my name and telephone number so you must have the right number. Might I ask where you got them from?'

'From your hire agreement form.' He swallowed some beer quickly and almost choked. What sort of game was she playing? If she didn't want the man with her to know what she'd been up to, which was obviously not an innocent visit to Mum, why continue the conversation?

'But I've never hired a car from you. There's nothing wrong with the one we have.' Jane Stevenson almost hung up then, until she remembered that she had left her car overnight in the underground car-park on Friday after that business with her handbag; although George had a spare key she hadn't felt like collecting it that evening. Could he possibly mean that? Could he even be the man who had taken her bag? Numerous scenarios flashed through her mind. Had he been stalking her and snatched her bag to find out all her personal details? Could he have something worse in mind? Maybe he had had copies of the keys made. Well, it was too late now, all the locks had been changed. She would not be intimidated. 'Look, I honestly don't know what all this is about but I think it might be an idea if you paid us a visit.' And then I'll know what you look like and so will George and we can take it from there.

'Are you sure?' Roger was taken aback. He, too, sensed something was very wrong.

'Yes. This evening, if it's convenient.'

'Certainly. I can be there in about half an hour.'

'That's fine. I take it you also know the address,' she added drily before hanging up.

Jane Stevenson turned to her husband, her attractive face creased with concern as she outlined the details of the conversation.

George shook his head. 'You can bet your life this is to do with your handbag. You did the right thing. We'll have a good look at this chap and take it from there. So much for an evening in the garden together.'

'There'll be other nights.' Jane smiled. 'Garden. Honestly, George. A few square feet of concrete, one flower-bed and a few pots.' But there was just enough room for two kitchen chairs where they could sit and catch the evening sun which, having moved round to the side of the house, shone directly into the yard.

'I know, but I've been thinking. Supposing we moved. Got a place with a proper garden. I couldn't do the heavy stuff, but I could learn how to fiddle around with plants and things. Not away from Rickenham Green, though. I know you wouldn't want that. Anyway, we'll talk about it later.'

Jane nodded. Moving had not crossed her mind. It might be just the thing to get George interested in life again.

Roger Pender was punctual. He pulled up almost outside the house, whose front door opened on to the pavement, got out of the car and rang the bell.

'Mr Pender?' Jane Stevenson stared at him. Yes, his face was vaguely familiar. She must have seen him on the forecourt on one of the many occasions she passed the garage on her way to work. 'I'm Jane Stevenson.'

'Oh.'

'Oh?' She glanced at him quizzically. He had sounded disappointed.

'You're not the same lady who hired the car from me.'

'I know that. Come in, please.'

He followed her out to the kitchen where she introduced him to her husband.

'Beer or something?' George asked gruffly, realising he was jealous of this younger, better-looking man with the thick head of hair who was showing an interest in his wife.

'Beer would be great, thank you.'

Jane poured three glasses and they sat at the kitchen table. 'What's all this about, Mr Pender?'

'On Friday evening a woman came into reception and asked to hire a car for the weekend. She said her own had broken down and she was going to visit her mother overnight. Naturally I had to see her driving licence and take her name, address and telephone number. All this I did. She gave the impression she lived alone and, to be honest, I thought she was coming on to me a bit. I liked her, she was open and friendly, or so I thought, and I wanted to see her again.' Roger noticed the look which passed between husband and wife but did not know what to make of it.

'How did she pay?' George inquired.

'Cash, actually. Seventy-five pounds in notes. It's not usual but it's more common than most people imagine.'

'And what time would this have been?'

'Around seven. A bit before, in fact. Why?'

'Because my wife had her handbag stolen on Friday evening. That would've been an hour or so before that woman came into your place.'

'You think this person I met took it?'

'It seems the logical answer.'

'Oh, hell, I'm so sorry.' Roger wondered whether he ought to offer to refund the cash. He had been taken in by a beautiful con artist. 'If I'd known the money was stolen it would have been a different matter. I'd never have hired her a car.'

'You couldn't have known. Anyway, it wasn't stolen, at least not from me. Nothing was taken. George found the bag hanging on the back door on Tuesday. It was soaking wet so it must've been hanging there for some time, possibly overnight. I'd cancelled the credit cards and we had the locks changed on Friday, so it wasn't a problem. But nothing was missing, that really surprised us.'

'If what you say is right, then someone took it deliberately to use a false identification.'

'What did she look like, this woman?'

'Slim, attractive, about late thirties was my initial guess until I saw the driving licence which told me, presumably wrongly, that she was forty-three. I think we ought to let the police know,

Mrs Stevenson. We don't know what we might be dealing with here.'

Jane sighed. George stood up and patted her shoulder. 'I agree with Mr Pender. We don't know what else she might get up to using your name, and if she's done or is still doing something illegal using your documents, you could end up in trouble, and so could our friend here if one of his vehicles was used in a crime.'

'You're right. Shall I do it?' Jane went to the telephone and dialled the number. 'Someone will be here as soon as possible,' she told them, once she had finished the call.

They used the time while they waited to talk about their lives and, feeling themselves to be united in a strange situation, began to use each other's first names. George began to like the man he had viewed vaguely as a threat to his marriage and asked, tentatively, whether he needed any help around the garage. He could drive a car through the washer, he said, without causing himself any damage. 'Don't think I'm after a job, Roger. I wouldn't need paying. I just need something to get up for in the mornings, something to get me out of the bloody house.'

'Consider it done.' Roger reached across the table and shook George's hand. 'Why not start tomorrow? But you can't do it for nothing. In return I'll get your car MOT'd and serviced along with all of mine. Will that suit?' He could see he had made two people very happy.

Jane smiled widely. It would certainly save her some money, but Roger Pender might also have saved their marriage. Whoever had taken her handbag had inadvertently done them a favour.

As he got out of bed Ian could hear the radio playing downstairs. Moira's side of the bed was cold. She had been up for some time. He showered and shaved and went down to see what effects the drink had had on his wife.

She stood at the sink, her back to him, a cup of tea in her hand. 'Feeling all right?' he asked gruffly, still annoyed that he had not been able to talk to her last night.

Moira turned round. 'Yes. Fine, thanks.'

And she looked it. Life wasn't fair. Her eyes were clear, her face was composed and her hands didn't tremble. She showed none of the signs of a hangover which afflicted him after a heavy night. 'Well, you don't deserve to.'

'Pots and kettles, darling,' she said sweetly. 'Tea or coffee?'

'Tea, please.'

'There's a postcard from Mark,' Moira said, wondering how it could have arrived so quickly when a letter she had written to her mother had taken five days to reach her by second class post. She placed it on the kitchen table in front of Ian who was sipping his tea morosely. 'What're you thinking? Still worried about the Graham case?'

'What?'

'I asked if work was worrying you?'

'Yes and no. Actually I was wondering what happened to my cigarette cards.' It was true, and he had not got there via a very complicated route. One of Malcolm Graham's hobbies had been pornography. Ian's pursuits had always been harmlesss, things which caused no shame or pain. As a child he had collected marbles and carefully stored the cards from his father's cigarette packets. As an adult he watched football, more precisely, Norwich City, the Canaries. What made a man like Graham do what he had done? Why, when he was good-looking, wealthy, well set-up and with a job he enjoyed, did he need whatever buzz he got from taking pictures of young girls?

Moira shrugged. There were times when her husband's line of thought eluded her. 'If they're anywhere they'll be in a box in the attic. Why?' August, Moira realised. The start of the football season proper. How could she have forgotten? But she was wrong, for once she had not been attuned to his thoughts.

'No reason. I wouldn't like to lose them, that's all. There's one of Bernard Robinson.'

'I can take it he played for Norwich,' she said drily.

The look on Ian's face made Moira smile. It was a mixture of disbelief and scorn. 'All right, of course he did. But I'm sorry, I've never heard of him.'

'No. Before your time. And mine too, actually. My father used to talk about him. Played for the Canaries for sixteen or seventeen seasons, 360 times in all.'

'I didn't know your father followed Norwich.'

'He didn't. He followed every team, didn't care who they were as long as they played football. He could name every player and which position they played in.'

Moira was losing interest. When the conversation turned to football her mind switched off. But it was the first time she had heard Ian speak of his father with anything resembling pride. He had been a stern, hard man, unable to show whatever feelings he might have possessed. As an only child with two such parents, it was amazing that Ian had weathered the storm and become the man he was. She turned to pour herself another cup of tea then opened the window wider as the first rays of sunshine came around the side of the house. It would be another hot day. 'What's brought this on? You haven't mentioned those cards for years.'

'I know. I'd always hoped Mark would be interested in sport. I kept them for him, really. They might even be worth something one day. I never imagined I'd have an artist as a son, or a French girl as a daughter-in-law, come to that. And I thought, well, now that he's married he'll probably have children and one of them might possibly be interested in those cards.' How did I get on to that? he wondered. I was thinking of Malcolm Graham.

They were now aware that payments into Graham's bank and building society accounts were made from two sources: his salary from Brockham's into the former and, periodically, differing amounts of cash into the latter. This made Alan Campbell's theory more realistic.

And, however unlikely it might seem, there was still the tiniest possibility that Graham had not locked his door and that some passing psychopath had taken a chance and popped in for a bit of Saturday night mutilation. There might even be someone from Graham's past they knew nothing about who had turned up. One thing was certain, they weren't getting any closer to the killer.

Moira, unaware of the turn of his thoughts, said nothing. Mark had always been artistic, never really one of the crowd, and before Yvette there had been an Italian girl. Neither of the things Ian had been unable to imagine had surprised her at all. She hoped he wasn't in for another disappointment. Mark and Yvette might not want children and if they did she could not imagine a modern child being interested in cigarette cards from the 1930s and '40s. 'I'll have a look for them later,' she said. 'Do you want any breakfast?'

'No. I don't think I've got time, love. Will you be in this evening?' There was a plaintive note to his question.

'Yes, I will. Honestly, you make it sound as if I'm out every night.' She paused on her way upstairs. 'Ian, was Mark such a disappointment to you?'

He met her eyes and smiled sadly. 'No, of course not. It was me that was a disappointment to him. I never really understood him, you see. I should not have hoped for or expected a replica of myself.'

Moira went back to him and kissed the top of his head. 'You two might not have much in common but he still loves you, you know. Now bugger off to work and let me get ready.'

Ian decided to walk. He had used the car every day recently and was becoming lazy again. As he made his way through the suburban streets, the warmth of the sun on his back, he thought back over the interview with Diane Hicks.

She still claimed she had no alibi and remained unconcerned by it. 'Look, Chief Inspector,' she had said, 'I can't prove one way or another where I was any more than I can prove I didn't know where he worked or where he lived. In fact, I still don't know where he lived, other than it's a Frampton address and that's only because you told me.'

'Did you telephone him on Saturday night from a call box in Saxborough?' Not knowing his address did not mean she did not know his phone number.

'I did not. I have a telephone at home and I have had nothing to say to that man for more years than I care to remember.'

'One of your daughters then?'

She had laughed at that. 'One lives in Devon, but she's in Majorca with her husband and children at the moment. The other one lives in London. I think it's highly unlikely that either of them crept back here, unobserved and unmissed by their respective families, and did such a thing, don't you?'

Eddie Roberts had been wrong about Diane Hicks's reasons for remaining so close to Rickenham Green. Her daughters had moved away but Diane ran her own business in the town. 'Did you kill your husband, Miss Hicks?'

'No, I did not. Look, you can do whatever you feel necessary to check on my movements but I cannot provide you with any proof of where I was on Saturday night. The world has changed, Chief Inspector. I can't even give you a detailed account of the television programmes I watched now that video recorders exist because I have one, you see, and there's nothing to prove I didn't watch them later.'

And Ian had believed her. Except she still had a motive. He had brought it up. 'We're still checking, Miss Hicks, but it seems more than likely that the will your husband made back in 1965 remains valid.'

'I had no idea he'd made one. He didn't tell me.' She had looked genuinely surprised, but nowhere near as surprised as when she learned that Malcolm Graham had left everything to her. 'What? Everything?'

'Yes.'

'My God. I would love to think it was true, Chief Inspector, but I bet you'll find another one. He could be very vindictive. But if you're right, then all I can say is that at least he had one redeeming feature if that's the way he wanted things.'

'Did you hate him that much?'

'No, not hate. I loved him at first, despite the way he was, moving from job to job, always saying it was someone else's fault he couldn't get on. Maybe Brockham's was what he was looking for. I'll never know now, of course. And then, when the children came, he changed. He stayed out more, he said their noise got on his nerves. Maybe that's why he lived alone afterwards, maybe he wasn't meant to live with anyone.' She paused. 'His main downfall was his mother. She was so bitter when he married me. I don't know whether it's in the genes or whether he learned his ways from her but they both had an enormous desire for power, a desire to control people. In Malcolm's case, people weaker than himself.'

'Miss Hicks, did he ever touch your daughters?'

'I told that other man, DC Roberts, he slapped them. Well, I did, too, when they deserved it, but on the hand or the legs and not hard. He did so too often and too harshly.'

That was not what Ian had meant. 'Sexually. Did he ever interfere with them in that way?'

She had looked away, her lips pressed together, then she looked back. 'No. I didn't like the things he did to me in bed, but

I'd never ever have allowed him near them if I'd believed that.'

'Is that why you moved out?' Ian had asked gently. 'Did you think it might come to that in the end?'

'Yes.' Her embarrassment was obvious. 'They were starting to grow up. Malcolm took more interest in them. I had a feeling I knew the reason why. That's when I got out. I asked them, you know, when they were grown up, but they both said nothing had ever happened.'

They had let her go then. There was no proof, nothing to say that Diane Hicks had not gone to Frampton on Saturday night and murdered the man who had misused her sexually then mutilated him in such a way that made it clear what she thought of his sexuality. Yet the three officers in the room with her at the time of her interview had had no doubt that she was innocent . . .

Ian had reached the station. 'Morning, sir.' The desk sergeant had a sheet of paper in his hand. 'WPC Saunders thought you might be interested in this.'

'Thanks.' Ian took the piece of paper and wondered what the Ice Maiden had come across that she thought might be important.

'Oh, for God's sake, Alan. Get real.'

Ian could hear Brenda Gibbons' voice from the end of the corridor. He walked faster. For her to be shouting at the innocuous Alan Campbell the matter must be serious.

'I don't need to get real, as you put it. I've bloody well lived through it,' he shouted back.

Ian pushed open the door of the general office. The eyes of the other detectives went back to their screens or whatever else they should have been doing. Brenda and Alan faced each other. Brenda was flushed, Alan bright red, his hands in fists at his sides. 'What's going on?' Ian's voice was deceptively smooth. Fight, by all means, but not in full view of everyone else thus giving people a chance to take sides.

'Nothing, sir.' Alan answered. Brenda appeared too incensed to speak.

'I hardly think screaming at one another is nothing. Let's go and talk about it, shall we?' He turned away, expecting them to follow, which they did.

In his own office he shut the door and asked them to sit down. 'Who's going first?' Neither spoke. 'Look, we've got crimes to solve, we can't sit here like an infant school class.'

Brenda flung her shiny hair back over her shoulders and smoothed down her cotton skirt. 'It was my fault, sir, I started it. Alan ... DC Campbell, wouldn't have it that a woman killed Graham. He seemed to think that women weren't capable of such things. I'd forgotten, I didn't think, sir –' She stopped mid-sentence, not wanting to say that she'd heard all about Alan's wife even though it was before she joined the team at Rickenham Green.

'Alan?'

His face was once more pale, untouched by the sun which he avoided. 'DC Gibbons misunderstood me, sir. I did not say I didn't think a woman was capable of such an act, I was simply trying to point out that we mustn't get entrenched in one way of thinking. There's absolutely nothing to say that a man didn't kill him.'

Ian saw how the argument had come about. Brenda, fiercely independent, fighting for a place in a man's world, in a man's job, as she saw it, wanted it to have been a woman, wanted the motive to be of the 'pay the bastard back' type. Alan, who surely did know what women were capable of, was merely being his usual pedantic self, taking all possibilities into consideration but without being able to express his ideas articulately.

Ian looked down at his desk. They were calmer now but this was a problem they would have to sort out for themselves. Tempers were beginning to fray, it was natural enough, it came with the job. Frustration built up with an absence of suspects and forensic evidence and motives which were only guessed at.

Without being aware of it he had read the note the desk sergeant had handed him.

'We're wasting time here. I want you to go and see these people and compare notes. Brenda, you go and see this Jane Stevenson and her husband. Alan, I want you at Pender's Garage.' He explained why and watched them leave.

*   *   *

107

Elaine Pritchard's sister had arrived on Wednesday night. She had dropped the children at her mother's but stayed chatting for longer than she had intended so there had been little chance for a proper conversation on Marion's first night as Elaine was tired. 'I'm so glad you're off tomorrow,' she said as they got ready for bed. 'It's ages since I've seen you.'

Elaine was glad, too. She was tired all the time lately. Having Thursday off meant working on Saturday but it made little difference. The days were all the same to her now.

'You look pale, didn't you sleep?' Marion asked as they sat outside the following morning drinking their first cup of coffee of the day. The bungalow had a large garden, mostly lawn. They sat at a round plastic table on matching white chairs.

'I haven't slept well for a long time.'

Marion, so like her to look at, reached over and patted her hand. 'It takes time, Elaine. It's only a year.'

'I know. It's not just Anna, at least I know she's not suffering any more, it's Brian, too. Sometimes when I come home after work and walk into this empty bungalow I feel like screaming. God, self-pity, how I hate it. I've let my friends drift out of my life, I've no one to blame but myself.'

'You didn't hear me, did you? It's a year, Elaine, twelve months. It takes far longer than that to repair your life. You've suffered two major losses in a very short time. Just do what you have been doing, take one day at a time and one day things will get better.' But not for me, not if what I believe is true, she thought.

'You're right. And if I don't shut up I'll spoil your visit. Shall we go somewhere? The beach perhaps? It's a shame to waste such a hot day.'

'The beach sounds great. Shall we take a picnic, like we did when we were kids?'

Elaine smiled. 'Lemonade and chocolate cake?'

'Acutally I was thinking along the lines of pâté, fruit and a bottle of wine. Is that delicatessen on the corner still in business? Good. You get dressed and I'll buy the food.' She found she was shaking as she reached for her bag.

'It was a blue Ford,' Alan Campbell told Ian. 'Paid for in cash.

Pender says he'd recognise the woman any day, not that he'd ever seen her before that evening.'

'Good.' The colour fitted with the description of the car seen parked in the gateway near Malcolm Graham's house. Ian was studying a copy of the hire agreement form which Alan had brought back with him. There was a signature, that of Jane Stevenson, but not the Jane Stevenson whose bag had been stolen. 'We'll see what Brenda has to say and take it from there.'

Jane had rung her office to explain why she would not be in until later in the morning. She and George answered all Brenda's questions as truthfully as they were able. 'I honestly couldn't say. There was the usual crowd of after-work customers, but they were at the bar all the time, and a few other people I hardly noticed. But there was one woman, she wasn't there when I came back from the Ladies, but I wasn't really concentrating. I couldn't describe her. She wasn't that young, that's all I really remember. That half-hour or so in the pub was precious to me, a few minutes to gather my thoughts, if you like. But nobody stood out. I mean, you know if someone's watching you.'

'No other younger female on her own?'

'Someone like me, you mean?' Jane smiled. 'Not that I noticed, but, as I said, I wasn't really looking. You don't think someone has used my name to do something dreadful?' The police had been around last night, the same two who had brought her home from the Coach and Horses. It had only just occurred to her that it seemed unnecessary for the CID to be following up the theft of a handbag, especially one that had been returned, its contents intact.

'We're not certain yet. Thankfully you reported the missing bag immediately, it's saved time on our part and any awkwardness on yours.'

Jane frowned and reached for the pot of coffee on the low table in front of them. The front room was cool, the slatted blinds lowered to keep out the glare. 'Is this anything to do with that man from Brockham's?'

'There's a possibility, but no more than that at the moment.' Brenda sipped the coffee. It was delicious. If offered, she would not refuse a second cup.

'How odd. I rarely shop there but I went in recently.'

Brenda looked up. Was there, after all, going to be a connection? 'When?'

'I popped in one lunchtime. Tuesday, that's when it rained, wasn't it? It's my daughter-in-law's birthday tomorrow. She's heavily pregnant and I wanted to buy her a treat. Some perfume. More than I'd normally pay, but she's not had an easy pregnancy.'

'Is there anyone you know who works at Brockham's?'

Jane shook her head. 'No. No, not really.' Elaine Pritchard didn't count, she was just a casual acquaintance from their days at the hospital.

'Daughter-in-law?' Brenda asked.

'Pardon?'

'Sorry. It's your son's wife who is having the baby?'

'Yes.'

'Have you any daughters?'

'No.' Jane thought the interview was over and that the lovely, fresh-faced policewoman was making conversation over the last of the coffee. 'We had two boys, then we tried a third time for a girl. No luck. Son number three arrived. But we're proud of them all. Are you married?' Jane blushed. It was far too intimate a question to have asked.

'I was. It was a disaster. But there's someone else now.' Andrew. Andrew, who was the only person able to rid her of the sour taste which lasted throughout a murder inquiry. Brenda stood up. 'I have to get back. If there's anything else you can think of, please let us know.' She stopped. 'The bag was hanging on the back door?'

'Yes.'

'Can you show me?' Brenda followed Jane out to the kitchen and into the yard. The handle was large enough for the bag to have remained in place whatever the weather. Yes, it would have had to have been the back. The front door opened directly on to the street. Whoever returned it would have been spotted immediately or the bag stolen for a second time. But to come in through someone's gateway was risky, especially as George was often at home. 'Do you lock the gate?'

'There isn't a lock.'

Brenda opened it. The hinges were oiled, it didn't squeak. Behind the houses ran a narrow lane. At night, hidden by the

110

high walls which protected the back yards, a person would not have been visible from the houses. 'Thanks. That's it. Can I get out this way?'

Brenda walked along the lane and took the alley which brought her back to the road.

The car was stifling. The visor was down but had offered no protection from the endless heat. The steering wheel was almost too hot to touch. She depressed a button which activated the windows and opened them all, then she indicated, checked her mirror and pulled out into the traffic.

Somebody honest, she thought, ironical as that sounded. If the same person who stole the bag also killed Malcolm Graham, they were basically honest or they'd have kept the money or chucked the whole lot in the river. Honest enough to have paid a night-time trip to return it, too.

Daughters. Why had she asked about daughters? Something along those lines had crossed her mind much earlier in the investigation, only she could not recall what, exactly. But all those girls and young women were somebody's daughters, women themselves, maybe, now. Maybe Alan Campbell wasn't far off the track, maybe a father had found out and put a stop to Graham's games. Yes, she owed Alan an apology. A man might leer at or ogle women other than his wife or girlfriend, he might even do more than that, but if his own daughter was interfered with, heaven help the culprit. God, she thought, long live hypocrisy.

She gritted her teeth, aware of her own vulnerability now. Yes, she could kill. The Ugly Brute, the Chief called him, but to her he was precious. It made her want to lash out. Words, but they had that effect. How, then, would she react if someone harmed him physically? It was a question better left unanswered.

Back at the station she joined Alan Campbell and reported what she had learned from Jane Stevenson. For no real reason she felt they were getting somewhere.

Forensics had towed the blue Ford away anyway. There might be something, the odd fibre, a single hair, a fingerprint that the vacuum cleaner or car-wash had missed. Or blood. Bloodstains might have been scrubbed clean, no longer visible to the naked eye, but there would still be traces, deep in the pile of the carpet. And they might find all of these things but they did not know if this was the car which had been parked in that gateway. They also did not know if the car in the gateway had anything to do with the murder of Malcolm Graham, but they couldn't take a chance.

'We'll get it back to you as soon as possible,' Alan had told Roger Pender. 'We do realise you had no way of knowing, and there might be a more innocent explanation. This woman, posing as someone else, could have had hundreds of reasons for hiring a car under a false name.'

Roger had nodded, but he was hurt and disillusioned. He had so much hoped to spend some time in the company of the person he had believed to be Jane Stevenson. 'All the cars are washed and valeted as soon as they're returned,' he'd repeated. The Ford had been no exception. A vehicle could not go out with a full ashtray or someone else's sticky finger marks on the steering wheel. It was amazing how many people ate or drank whilst they drove.

Brenda, Alan and the Chief were in the almost deserted general office trying to make something of this new development. They had a sighting of a blue car on the night of the murder and a blue Ford had been hired by someone using a stolen identity. Gradually the alibis of all those involved were being checked. Being a Saturday night, many of the staff at Brockham's had been out and had plenty of witnesses to vouch for their whereabouts. Those married with children had been at home with their families and some, the more solitary women like Elaine Pritchard, had gone to visit relatives. Mrs Pritchard had spent the night in Ipswich with her mother, Sheila Foster, who had been celebrating her birthday belatedly.

There was no sign of Scruffy Short who had disappeared an hour ago, or Eddie Roberts who had left a message to say he would not be long. Nor was there any more news from Frampton. The incident room was being packed up. Information had come in in dribbles which had soon dried up. Four days on from the discovery of the body and the locals were already losing interest. It wasn't their business, they had their own busy lives to lead, but now the gossip had taken a different slant, now it was along the lines of how he must have done something to deserve it, and wasn't it strange how no one had really known him.

Superintendent Thorne had drafted a brief statement which had been passed on to Martyn Bright, editor of the *Rickenham Herald*, the weekly paper which came out on Fridays. The story would appear in the morning. It told the public little more than they knew already. If the details of the murder were released they'd have even more nutters on the phone claiming responsibility than they were trying to cope with already.

It took the return of Eddie Roberts to lighten the mood of the three assembled detectives. In his hand was a large buff folder. 'They're back, the first batch of the photographs.' Before they were sent to the computer department there had been some painstaking work for several officers who had sifted through the originals, trying to recognise which ones were recent, which ones were not. Hairstyles were helpful in some cases, as were the furnishings in the background. In one there had actually been a calendar; the date, viewed through a magnifying-glass, showed that Graham's handiwork went back over twenty years. The computer operators had aged the women by varying degrees.

'Let's have a look, see if we can match any faces.'

As if his salacious nature was assisted by telepathy, John Short walked through the door, adjusting his flies as he did so. His face was pinker than usual and his eyes sparkled. Ian took one look at him and guessed, correctly, that he had spent his lunch break in the bed of the woman he was reportedly seeing. Not that she had ever been introduced to any of them. They did not even know her name. Married, most likely, he thought, wrongly, just as everyone else did.

113

'Aha, the nymphets in middle age. Let's have a look.' Short leaned on the table. It creaked beneath his weight. His breath smelled of onions.

They fanned out the photographs, interested to see what the experts in such matters believed the women would now look like. The computer had done a remarkable job; the girls were still recognisable in the older faces and bodies of the women in front of them.

'Hang on, don't we know this lady?' Short picked up a photograph and studied it, sucking on his moustache as he did so. There was something very familiar about the woman yet something not quite right. Whoever he was thinking of was younger, or, at least, younger-looking, and surely her hair was a different colour now? He squinted, holding the picture away from him. Then he slung it on the table on top of the others and jabbed his forefinger in its centre, unconsciously stabbing the glossy bosom. 'That, I do believe, gentlemen, oh, and lady,' he nodded at Brenda, 'is none other than the lovely Miss Carmen Brockham.'

Brenda snatched up the picture and stared at it. 'This one was separate, this one was in the box of old bills. You could be right.'

'Trust me. I am.'

'The over-generous salary – was it hush money, do you suppose?' Brenda suggested.

'There's one way to find out. My turn, I think. Brenda, you'd better come too.' Ian was on his feet, his large frame blocking the light from the window. He rubbed his hands together as he always did when he was anticipating something new to work on.

'Ah, well, I knew I couldn't be lucky twice. But it gives her a motive, all right. All those years of paying him, all those years with this hanging over her. Maybe it's the reason she never married,' Short said as he put his feet on the desk, mindless that his shoes were scuffed and there was chewing-gum stuck to the sole of one of them. 'Looks like it's all sorted,' he said. 'That was the reason she asked if we'd searched the place. She knew exactly what we'd find. Strange there aren't any more of her.' He sniffed. 'It won't be her. Life's never that simple, not in this job.'

Ian was inclined to agree with the latter statement. It was such a long time ago. Why put up with it for twenty-odd years, why put up with it at all? Few people had nothing in their past of which they were ashamed. And from what he had heard about Carmen Brockham she did not seem the sort to fall in with Graham's revolting ways or to be taken in by the threat of blackmail. However, something in her circumstances might have altered, something which had acted as the catalyst leading to murder.

A cool breeze rippled through the heads of the roses in the beds at the front of the station, scattering yellow and white petals over the earth. Brenda got behind the wheel, aware that the Chief preferred being a passenger.

They drove to Collerton Manor through a mixture of weather. More like April than August, Ian thought as Brenda skilfully wound her way through the narrow lanes. Clouds passed overhead, their shadows flowing swiftly across the fields of ripened crops, some already cut and baled. Sudden showers hit the windscreen but did not last more than seconds. The sun came out and disappeared again behind a cloud. The cow parsley, high in the hedges, had been at its best until June but here and there a few white heads reflowered sporadically.

Ian made no comment as they approached the house. He had expected the Brockham family home to be impressive, and it was.

Carmen Brockham might have been expecting them, she opened the door so eagerly. She was wearing a tight-fitting dress. The material was slightly shiny and clung to her body, stopping just short of her knees. Her feet were encased in Italian leather sandals, her toenails painted pearly pink to match those of her hands. And in her hand was a glass. Hadn't he heard that her father was an alcoholic? Maybe it ran in the family. It was only mid-afternoon, a bit early to have started on the hard stuff.

'Please come in,' she said.

They followed her into the lounge and sat down, Brenda in one cream leather settee, Ian in the other. It was a light and spacious room, the furnishings all pale, the pictures on the wall tasteful and probably originals. Carmen placed her drink on the high shelf of the mantelpiece next to a flower-filled vase but she remained standing. 'Rather an exception, this,' she said in her mellifluous voice as she gestured towards the glass. 'Dutch courage, actually. I don't expect you to believe me, but I was just about to telephone you.'

'About what, Miss Brockham?'

'About Malcolm. What else? I have now had several days to think about this and I've decided that, whatever the consequences might be, you ought to hear what I have to say. But first, may I get you something? Tea, or a drink?'

'No, thank you.'

She smiled. It was a beautiful, self-deprecating smile. 'Ah, so I'm not to be given even a moment's reprieve.' It was a statement. 'Shall I just tell you in my own words how it was? I believe that's the way you put it.'

'Please do.' Ian tried not to smile back. He had never set eyes on the woman before but she was lovely and he liked her immediately; he sensed that whatever she did tell them, it would be the truth.

'I've known Malcolm for most of my life. He's older than me by fourteen years, so he was an adult when I was a child. My father introduced me to him, we were attending some function or other, I was only thirteen but Dad believed I should know how to conduct myself at such affairs from an early age. It was terribly boring but it stood me in good stead later.

'God knows how Malcolm got himself invited, but he's always been a social climber, a bit of a snob, actually. Later I learned he had always had a fascination with Brockham's. He didn't say, but I think as a child and a young man it represented the luxury he craved. He was a drifter when I met him, never staying in any job long, I didn't know until this week he was already married with one child and another on the way. But despite my father's guidance I was terribly naïve.

'For some reason he came to the house one day and we were alone for a few minutes. He told me I was beautiful, that I would make a wonderful model and that he could help me become one. But I wasn't to tell my father because he was sure to disapprove, which, of course, he would have done.' Carmen held out a hand. 'I know, it sounds old hat today. I was fourteen by then, no teenager would fall for it now. But he was twenty-eight and I had no experience of men or boys. I was flattered, it was the boost my ego needed. You know what it's like to be that age, all gawkiness and lack of confidence.' She had turned to Brenda, who nodded. Yes, indeed, she knew what it was like to be fourteen but she knew that that could be the only thing she had in common with Carmen Brockham who, probably even today, had no idea what an inner-city school looked like or what it was to live partly with foster parents and partly with an alcoholic mother. Money, servants, a big house and a private education, how very far from Brenda's sometimes violent, at best indifferent, upbringing. Or so she thought.

'I had no one to guide me, you see. My mother ran off with someone from the store when I was a baby. I never knew her. Dad did his best, he dragged me round the social scene with no real idea of who or what I was. He was an alcoholic, which didn't help matters, although he disguised it well. This drink,' she picked up the glass, 'this just isn't like me, but I needed it before I picked up the phone. However, you forestalled me.

'I was a lonely child, Chief Inspector, and, until now, a lonely woman.'

Carmen sat down and sipped the vodka and tonic. Her hand hardly shook but Brenda noticed the slight tremor. Was there anyone who had lived a happy life? she wondered, astonished at Miss Brockham's revelations. 'How did Malcolm come to work for you?'

'I was coming to that. You've probably guessed how things went. Malcolm hired a tiny room and took some photos, straight ones the first time. He said he was showing them to a modelling agency and if they took me on, he'd get commission. It sounded plausible to me, even at that age, especially as I knew he was short of money. A week or so later he said they were interested but they wanted some underwear shots. I was more confident by then. Well, you must know how things progressed. And, of course, there was no modelling agency. He kept those photographs. He said if I ever mentioned them he'd show them to my father who would disinherit me. I believed him.

'Nothing happened for a long time, not until Dad died and I took over the store. I'd almost forgotten about it by then. Malcolm came to me and asked for a job, the manager's job. He said if I refused him he'd pin the pictures up all over the store and send copies to the paper.' She shrugged. 'I gave him the job.

117

Okay, it sounds like yet another excuse but I was twenty-four and without much in the way of experience. What surprised me then was that he hadn't come directly to me for money. It was the job he wanted and the prestige he felt went with it.'

'Did he ever threaten you again?' Ian was leaning forward, his hands between his knees. He still didn't fully understand why she hadn't simply told him where to go. She had nothing to lose now.

'Not threaten, no. He just kept on asking me for a rise.'

'You could have refused him.'

'So I could, Chief Inspector, but old habits die hard. The pattern had emerged far too long ago. Tell me, did he really keep those photographs?'

'We found only one of you.'

'The way you phrased that makes me think there were other girls involved. How many people did he prey on?'

'Quite a lot.'

Carmen thought about this. 'So there are other people, apart from myself, who had good reason to wish him dead.'

Ian chose to ignore the last statement. 'What made you decide to tell us now?'

She looked down at her hands, which lay clasped in her lap to keep them still. 'I have met a man with whom I want to share my life. I love him. I have never loved anyone before and I think, at last, I can find some real happiness. Whether he would understand or not is beside the point, I'm willing to take that risk if I must. The risk I'm not prepared to take is what it would do to him if it came out. He's an MP, you see, and you know how the press love this sort of thing. Obviously you cannot jeopardise your case but if I knew no one would find out what I did – no, let me put it another way. If you cannot tell me categorically that there is no danger of anyone knowing, then I will tell Neil that I cannot marry him. He proposed to me last night, you see, but I didn't give him an answer.'

'You care for him that much?' Brenda asked, seeing yet another similarity between them. She would never endanger Andrew's career.

'I do. I also realise that by telling you I have become a suspect. You're probably thinking that I killed him to stop the blackmail, that I knew how vulnerable Neil would be and suddenly decided to put an end to it.' She smiled. 'However, had I been so inclined, I would've made damn sure I retrieved those photographs.'

'Miss Brockham, we had some idea of what went on and, I'm sorry, but for the moment we cannot give you any guarantee it won't come out.'

'I see,' she said quietly.

'Look, isn't there any way you can put off giving him an answer, a few days, maybe?' Ian felt sorry for her, a dangerous thing to do. She was a suspect.

'Yes, of course. I'll think of something.'

'Is there anything else you wish to tell us?'

Carmen bit her lip. 'Oh, God, life's a real bitch, isn't it? I suppose you ought to know, but I'm sure there's nothing in it.' She sighed. 'It seems so disloyal. And I'm not going to come out of this very well either.

'My assistant manager, Sylvie Harris, wrote me some anonymous letters concerning Malcolm. To be blunt, she was after his job. It was no secret, she told the staff she could do it just as well, if not better. And she made her feelings clear to me. She's good, but not as good as she thinks, and not as good as Malcolm was. Oh, I didn't mention that, did I? The arrangement wasn't entirely one-sided. Malcolm kept his side of the bargain, he was perfect for the job. He knew every member of staff, including the cleaners, he kept things running smoothly and staff disputes to a bare minimum. Anyway, I did wonder if Sylvie had been in the same position as myself. From those letters I gathered she knew the kind of man Malcolm was. She described him as perverted, a sexual menace, that type of thing, and suggested I get rid of him. I began to think he may have told her about me, they spent a fair amount of time together at work. Then I realised I was wrong. On one of my rare visits to Brockham's Malcolm told me he had gone to Sylvie's house and had sex with her. 'She was asking for it,' he told me. 'She's the sort that likes a bit of rough.' I didn't take a lot of notice really because it was obvious Sylvie had her eye on him. But I didn't know how cruel to her he had been. It was about this time the letters came and I guessed what had happened. She couldn't have the man so she'd take his job.'

'Why do you think he told you?'

119

'I don't know really. Perhaps in case she complained to me, but more likely to prove he was still virile. Maybe even because he had plans to play us off against one another. I really can't say. Well, that's it, Chief Inspector, I've told you everything I know or I think could be of use to you.'

'Miss Brockham, you have not been able to establish an alibi for yourself for the night Mr Graham was killed, at least, not after five thirty when the last of your house staff went home. Therefore I have to ask you, did you kill Malcolm Graham?'

'No. I did not. There were times when I wished for his death, especially recently, but no, I didn't kill him.'

Ian nodded. 'We might need to speak to you again and we'll need you to make a formal statement. One more thing, do you still have the letters Mrs Harris wrote to you?'

Carmen turned away, blushing. She had forgotten to destroy them. Malcolm had received some letters too, but this was one thing she would keep to herself because she was certain Sylvie had not written them. 'I do. I'll get them for you.' She left the room and returned a few minutes later. 'Just these. There were no more.'

'Thank you.' Ian glanced at them and put them in his pocket. The envelopes had been typed. The letters Graham had received had been handwritten, but he had not kept the envelopes. These envelopes, addressed to Carmen at home, might also contain handwritten messages, in which case Sylvie Harris was high up on the list of suspects. Graham, it seemed, had, as they suspected, rebuffed her. She was also after his job. She had sent anonymous letters to Carmen Brockham so was probably the author of those sent to Graham threatening him with death. 'How did you know Mrs Harris wrote them?'

'She admitted it to me. I know I ought to have said something before but I really didn't want to get her into unnecessary trouble. And now, I suppose, it looks as if I'm trying to place the blame elsewhere.'

'One last thing, Miss Brockham, do you know someone called Jane Stevenson?'

She shook her head. 'No, I've never heard of her.'

Had she been the one to steal the handbag or to use the false identity, there would have been some sign of guilt or nervousness, no matter how small. There was none.

'All or nothing,' Brenda commented as they walked to the car. 'Miss Brockham definitely had a lot to lose with Malcolm becoming more demanding and with the threat of him discovering her relationship with the MP. And she suddenly decides to produce those letters. She might've written them herself, to cover herself if we found the ones Graham received. But everything she said also puts Sylvie Harris high on the list.'

'Well, we'll find out, shall we?'

The next stop would be the department store. Brenda started the car and began the journey back to Rickenham Green. 'You'd never think it to look at her, would you?'

'What's that?' Ian's mind was elsewhere, he was hoping that Forensics would turn up something in the blue Ford, preferably Sylvie Harris's fingerprints. And Malcolm Graham's blood. O Rhesus Negative. The uncommon group made life so much easier when it came to comparing samples.

'That a woman like that had such a miserable past. It hasn't affected her looks, you have to give her that.'

Nor yours, Ian thought but did not say. He was fully aware of the background from which Brenda had come, and how she had made something of herself.

They were lucky, they found a space not far from Brockham's. Brenda parked neatly and locked the car. They walked beneath the racing clouds which cast buildings alternately in sunshine and in shadow towards the plate glass doors of Brockham's, behind which stood a bored-looking security guard.

Ian produced his identity. 'We'd like to speak to Mrs Harris, please. Where might we find her?'

'Top floor. If she's not in Mr Graham's office just ask one of the staff to page her for you. His name's on the door, you can't miss it.'

Brenda eyed the perfume but didn't touch the testers. Instead she said, 'I feel I deserve a discount the amount of times I've been in here recently.'

'Let's hope it's the last,' Ian said as they stepped on to the escalator.

Roger Pender was not expecting another visit from the police. It was a different man this time, one who introduced himself as

Detective Constable Roberts. 'I won't take up much of your time, I'd just like you to tell me if this could possibly be the woman who hired the car from you.' Eddie was aware that computer-enhancing was not infallible, and Scruffy Short had said the likeness was there but not terribly strong.

Roger looked at the artificially aged photograph of Carmen Brockham, a head and shoulders shot. 'No. I'm sorry, that's nothing like her. She was – well, softer-looking with beautiful eyes and a lovely smile. Nothing about her that really stood out, except maybe an aura of sadness. Don't ask me how I know, I just felt it. When she smiled it was genuine, though. God, it's so difficult to describe someone accurately, and I only saw her the once. But I'd know her immediately if I ever met her again.'

Eddie shivered. He was in shirt-sleeves, his jacket was back at the station. Overhead the flags snapped in the wind. He wondered if the noise drove Roger Pender mad in the winter. 'There's nothing else you can recall about her?'

'No. Sorry.'

He had already given them a description of hair colour and what she had been wearing. No jewellery, he had also noticed that much. Eddie now believed that this was deliberate; a necklace or earrings were often a give-away when it came to identification.

Roger watched the car drive off. He very much wanted to see the woman again, he very much wanted to know she was innocent.

'I enjoyed today,' Elaine told Marion when they returned to the house. Her face was flushed from the sun and the salty breeze which had sprayed them with sand. But in the hollows of the dunes, amongst the reeds, they had been sheltered. They had eaten and dozed and read and talked.

'It shows. In one day you look better already. Doesn't the sea air make you sleepy?' Marion yawned.

'Yes. And it's back to work for me tomorrow. Are you sure you'll be able to amuse yourself?'

'Of course. If it's sunny I'll laze in the garden. It's bliss to get away from the children for a day or so. Mum's a saint, offering to have them. God, I'm sorry, Elaine. That was a tactless thing to say.'

'It's all right. Honestly. I felt the same way when Anna was alive. Especially towards the end when her illness became progressively worse. It makes me feel guilty now, but the counsellor told me that was natural, that no matter how much I'd done for her, I'd still feel I could've done more.'

'I honestly don't know how you coped. You were wonderful with her, Elaine. And so was Brian, of course. Mum's always singing your praises.'

You're right, Mum is a saint, Elaine thought. She loves us both so very much, and the children. I know she wants to spend as much time as possible with the two surviving ones. They think I don't know how much it tires her, but I do. And I'll never forget all she did for Anna. Never. 'She sings your praises, too,' Elaine replied with a smile, recalling the birthday party where they had all drunk too much but thoroughly enjoyed themselves.

'What's so amusing?'

'I was thinking of Mum last Saturday. She put a few away, which isn't normally like her.'

'Ah, well, she deserves to relax occasionally. Are you ready for bed?' Marion got up. It had worried her, seeing her mother almost drunk, but maybe it was the combined effects of medication and alcohol.

'Yes. Go on, you can use the bathroom first.'

They lay in their separate bedrooms but neither woman slept well that night.

14

Ian tapped on the ridged glass in the door through which he could see the blurred outline of someone seated behind a desk. Screwed to the wood of the lower half of the door was a brass plaque bearing Malcolm Graham's name. No one had yet been heartless enough to remove it. But then, no successor had yet been appointed either. It would not be Sylvic Harris, Carmen Brockham had made that clear.

'Come in.' Sylvie's eyes widened in surprise when she saw the police were back again. She had already met the female detective but not the man with her. When she learned who Ian was her mouth went dry. For someone of such superior rank to wish to speak to her could only mean trouble. 'Won't you sit down?' Apart from her own there was only one other chair visible. Glad of movement, of a chance to prepare herself, Sylvie got up and fetched a third chair from the small ante-room off the office. 'What is it you want? It's about Malcolm again, I suppose?' she said with a touch of bitterness.

'Yes.' Ian appraised the woman. Thin and hard-faced, with, he suspected, a nature to match. Dressed in uncompromising and unflattering black, she resembled a crow.

'I've told you everything I can. I really don't see what a third interview can achieve. And, as you must surely appreciate, I'm extremely busy. There are still some staff holidays to sort out on top of everything else.'

Ian ignored all but her second remark. 'It's surprising how much we can learn from further interviews, Mrs Harris. Are you sure you've told us everything? You see, we know that Mr Graham received some threatening anonymous letters during the period just before he was killed. We also believe they were written by a woman.' They did not know either of those things. The letters had been undated. They might have been written years ago, but if so the paper was well preserved. However, the style indicated a female correspondent. If she had been their author she might believe that they already knew that and decide it was time to admit it. As yet there was no evidence regarding fingerprints or where the paper may have been purchased. It might be necessary to fingerprint everyone they had spoken to if Forensics came up with any positive sets on the paper.

'You have my word that I did not write them.' Sylvie bit her lip. Scarlet lipstick left a stain on her teeth. These people were here because they knew something. It would be better to find out just how much. 'All right. There is something. You'll never believe me, not now. I did write some letters but they were to Carmen. Miss Brockham.'

'Why?' Ian was pleased the woman did not know Carmen had already told them so. If both parties turned out to be innocent it would save embarrassment all round.

'Malcolm hated me. He made my life here a misery. He was getting on, he was sixty, but he refused to retire, and he could well have afforded to. He was paid far more than the job was worth. I thought if Carmen knew what sort of a man he was, she'd make him take early retirement. I knew she wouldn't sack him, not after twenty-two years.'

'What sort of a man was he, Mrs Harris?'

It was Brenda she looked at when she replied, as if she was sure another woman would understand her position better. 'I think I told you before that he was brutal, crass and ego-centric.'

'He hit you?' It was the first time Brenda had spoken. She had seen the slight inclination of the Chief's head and knew he wanted her to take over.

'Good heavens, no.' The redness in Sylvie's face clashed with her lipstick.

'Then how do you mean?'

'We had an affair.'

Brenda and Short had guessed that much but it was not what Carmen Brockham had led them to believe. 'Did it last long?'

'I – well, no. No, it didn't. At the time I believed that that was his intention, that we'd become a couple. I didn't know him as well as I thought I had.'

'How long were you seeing him out of office hours?' Brenda asked gently, already knowing the answer.

Sylvie looked away, ashamed and embarrassed. 'Just the once. He came to my house. He – oh, God. It was like being raped. It was horrible. I'd prepared a meal and bought wine, but he didn't wait for that. It was all wasted. At first I thought he was nervous. Afterwards he laughed and he said some horrible things to me.'

'What sort of things?'

'That I'd been asking for it, and now I'd had it. And did I really think he'd . . .' She paused, catching her breath at the renewed pain. 'Did I think he could possibly be interested in a shrivelled-up old cow like me. After that he'd just grin at me every time our paths crossed. It was awful, knowing what he was thinking. It was driving me mad.'

Ian felt sorry for her. Here was a woman of a certain age who made every effort to look seductive and who had failed. Perhaps

125

she had considered Malcolm Graham to be her last chance. To have been used, then spoken to in that manner, must have been devastating, especially when she had to work alongside the man. But was it reason enough to have killed him?

It was Brenda who verbalised his thoughts. 'So you killed him?'

'No, Miss Gibbons. I did not. But I very much wish that I had done. It would have given me great pleasure to see that man suffer.'

'Do you know anyone by the name of Jane Stevenson?'

'No, I'm sorry, I don't.' The change of tactic did not confuse her. The answer came easily, the response sounded genuine.

'Did you hire a car over last weekend?'

'Whatever for? I have my own car, not that I use it very often.'

'The make and colour?' They had seen Carmen's car. A white Audi. It would have been noticeable if she had driven it through Frampton.

'It's a red Datsun. I bought it second-hand from Pender's Garage two years ago. Why?'

Pender's Garage. Did it mean anything? Probably not. The place was well patronised because of its good reputation. 'A car was seen near Mr Graham's house on the night he died.'

Sylvie's expression relaxed a little. 'Well, it wasn't mine. My car was parked in the drive the whole weekend. You can ask any of my neighbours. I live in a cul-de-sac, it's crescent-shaped, we can all see each other's drives.'

They would ask her neighbours, of course. But they might not have noticed if she'd slipped out while they were eating dinner or watching television.

'Did you know how much Mr Graham earned?'

'Not exactly.' She frowned. 'Is it relevant?'

Ian shook his head. If she had known and was after his job it might have been. 'Mrs Harris, we'd like you to make a statement. Is there someone you can trust to lock up when the store closes?'

'No. I'm afraid not. Only Malcolm and I hold keys. Carmen wouldn't have it any other way. It would be far too risky.'

'But surely, since he's dead, someone else has been allocated as the second key-holder?'

126

'No. I imagined you'd have the other set. Malcolm would have taken them home with him.'

In that case they were still at the house. There had been three bunches of keys hanging on hooks in the kitchen. He would have to arrange for them to be returned to Miss Brockham. 'Then, if you wouldn't mind, we'd like you to call in after work, on your way home.'

Sylvie said she would do so.

Ian and Brenda paused in the doorway. Brenda turned to him and spoke quickly and softly. Ian nodded his agreement.

'Mrs Harris, are the personnel records kept here?' Brenda asked.

'Yes. The old ones are in the filing cabinet, but for the past couple of years everything's been logged on the computer.'

'Would it take you long to make a list of all the staff who have children?'

'No. About five minutes, I should think.'

'Could you do so, please?'

They all sat down again. Ian was surprised the woman had not asked why they should want this. But Brenda had a point. Maybe someone who worked at Brockham's had a daughter who had fallen into Malcolm Graham's hands. They were back on the same track: if not one of the girls, now a woman, seeking revenge or trying to escape from blackmail, then one of the girls' parents.

Sylvie pressed a button and the machine spewed out several sheets of paper. She stapled them together.

'Thank you.' Ian took the printed pages and ran his eye down them swiftly. There were fewer names than he had expected but many of the staff were young, not yet married. He would study the list properly back at the station.

'She could have done it. Did you see the expression on her face when she described that evening?' Brenda did not think she had witnessed such obvious hatred before.

'Maybe. She was hurt and humiliated but she struck me as the sort of woman who would get back at him in spiteful ways, such as writing those letters. And there's something else.'

Brenda unlocked the car and they got in. 'Something else?'

'He was naked. His clothes were undamaged, therefore he had taken them off before he was killed. Now, unless whoever did it asked him to, at knife-point, which is unlikely as they were neatly folded over the back of the chair, the logical conclusion is that this was prior to having sex. Your theory of it being a woman still looks good, but not Mrs Harris, she wouldn't subject herself to such humiliation a second time.'

'Maybe not sex. Maybe a man forced him to undress. Graham would probably have dropped his clothes on the floor then the killer, maybe knowing what a meticulous person he was, folded them neatly afterwards. It's what I'd do if I wanted to confuse the evidence. And the post-mortem showed no sexual inter-course had taken place.'

'Mm.' Ian said no more. He was smiling to himself. Brenda did not believe what she had said – she was convinced it was a woman. This was her way of making amends, of accepting that Alan Campbell had a point. No one knew for certain the gender of the killer. A woman could use a knife as well as a man, especially as Malcolm Graham had traces of barbiturates in his blood. Just enough to slow him down, to give his murderer the edge.

'Anything new?' he asked when they were back in the general office.

Eddie Roberts had been over to Saxborough and questioned Diane Hicks's neighbours. As far as they were aware she had been at home on the relevant Saturday evening. 'The plumbing's noisy here, it's the same in all of these houses. You get to know each other's habits quite well,' one of them said. 'I heard bath-water running about nine. And later, the toilet being flushed. She doesn't go out much. I don't think she's got many friends.'

'How much later did you hear the toilet flushing?' Eddie had asked.

'It would've been about ten thirty, I think. Diane's an early riser. She's got her own greengrocery business and has to be there for the delivery vans before she opens up, so she doesn't stay up late. And she has to take the dog out first.'

Eddie had not been aware of a dog in the house but it had probably been shut in the kitchen. No watchdog then, but a pet because it certainly hadn't barked the evening he had knocked on the door. 'So she goes to bed early even on Saturdays?'

'Yes. Same routine. Out with the dog morning and evening,

work all week and then she potters about in the garden on Sundays if the weather's fine.'

And the neighbour the other side had seen her with the dog walking past his house at a few minutes past seven the following morning. It meant nothing, she could still have killed her husband, but what he learned fitted in with what Diane Hicks had told them. If it wasn't for the fact that she was the sole beneficiary in her husband's will it was doubtful they would be wasting their time checking her movements now.

'So,' Ian concluded, 'I want all the people on this list interviewed again. They're all staff at Brockham's and they've all got children. Stick to those with daughters and ignore the ones with small ones, the ones at an age when they wouldn't be left unsupervised, and concentrate on the others. Regardless of which parent works at the store, speak to them both.' He glanced at the clock on the wall. 'Sylvie Harris is coming in to make a statement, she should be here any minute. Meanwhile, we'll get started on this. People should be arriving home from work by now.'

There were over thirty names on the list who had daughters, only a small proportion of the total number of staff Carmen Brockham employed, but more than three each. They would not get through them all in one night.

John Short scanned his copy. 'Best do it in areas,' he said. 'If we each take the ones who live closest to each other we'll save a bit of time.' He was disappointed. Elaine Pritchard was not one of them. Divorced, she had said during her interview, and now he knew by the absence of her name from the list that she was childless. No complications. Maybe later, maybe after this case was concluded, if it ever was, he'd call into Brockham's and ask her advice about after-shave. Not that he'd ever wear any, but it was a way of getting to know her. He felt no shame. Lunchtime with Nancy was light years away.

Within a few minutes, after consulting the map of Rickenham Green, they were on their way.

'He had to have known whoever killed him,' Moira said, half listening to Ian, one eye on the television. It was no good. He wanted to talk, it helped him unwind, and she'd lost the thread of what she had been watching. She got up and switched off the set. Having earlier indulged in one of her favourite pastimes – a long bath with a book and a glass of wine balanced on the corner of the bath – she was in her nightclothes, a matching nightdress and short-sleeved robe of cream satin. They were new. Ian did not notice. Moira was used to it. It was strange, though: for a policeman he was extremely unobservant at home. She moved away from the television. The robe fell open. Still he did not notice. She shrugged mentally and sat down.

'We've always assumed that. There was no forced entry, there-fore he let his killer in, and, presumably, he was expecting whoever it was.' They still had no idea who had made that last telephone call.

'You told me all that before. I meant really known them, for him to have been lying on the bed naked. What you were saying, about being forced to do so, I just can't see it. I mean, if you're threatened at knife-point, especially by a woman, who you'd probably think was weaker than you, you wouldn't take it lying down. You'd . . . What? What is it?'

Ian had shaken his head. 'Not you too.'

'Pardon?'

'Clichés. I get enough of that from Scruffy Short.'

'Actually, Ian, if you mean my saying "lying down", it's more of a pun. Anyway, you'd put up some sort of a fight, at least struggle if not refuse to lie down in the first place. I think he believed he really was going to have sex. And do you know what else I think?'

'Go on.'

'That this woman also took off her clothes. That way she wouldn't get any blood on them. Maybe she showered after-wards. I don't know. Don't you check the plugholes for blood or something?'

'We do, and we did.'

'And?'

'And nothing. But what you say makes sense. If she – if it was a she – was also naked, he'd have no cause for suspicion. This woman must be extremely cold-hearted and very calculating. And you, Moira Roper, have a much nastier mind than I gave you credit for. I like the nightie, by the way.'

'Thank you.' She looked up at him with surprise. He was

grinning. She realised then that he had noticed it as soon as he came in. How very much younger he looked when he smiled.

'Now be a good wife and get me a beer. I forwent the pleasures of the Crown to get home to you.'

'Ian, you've mentioned all this thing with the young girls. Could it be a cover-up?' she said when she returned with the beer.

'In what way?'

'Maybe he was trying to kid himself, convince himself, if you like, that that was what men did, what he ought to be doing. He never had girlfriends, you said, no relationships after the one with his wife, and even then the sex was abnormal. Maybe he preferred men. You see, it crossed my mind that whoever was there with him might have been a regular visitor, one who came late at night so the neighbours wouldn't know, especially if it was another man.'

Ian sighed as he leaned his head against the back of the armchair. 'Then that would mean all our efforts have been wasted. If it was a male it could be someone he'd picked up over the past twenty-odd years or a week or so ago, someone we know nothing about.'

'I should've kept quiet. I've made things worse. Anyway, I still think it's a woman. Only a female would mutilate someone in that way.'

'Could you do it?'

Moira pushed her hair behind her ears but it was so soft from being recently washed that it fell straight back over her face. 'I don't know. I don't think anyone knows what they are capable of until circumstances take over. I know when Mark was little I thought I'd kill anyone who touched him. Probably I still would. But to do that? I'm not sure. Could you?'

'No. I can honestly say I could not. Come and sit on my knee and make an old man happy. I'm sick of the whole thing. There just doesn't seem anywhere else to turn.' And those sums of money, paid into his account in cash. It had to be blackmail. He put an arm around Moira and held his glass in the other hand. Between them they'd seen ten of the people on the list, and their partners, those who had them. One was a single mother, another was divorced. They had come up with nothing.

'Ian.' Moira reached for his glass and grabbed it before it fell to the floor. Ian, his head on her shoulder, had fallen asleep.

'It's all right. I only had my eyes closed,' he said.

'Bed. You're exhausted. And I'm tired, too.'

Moira checked the doors and windows were locked and went upstairs. Ian was asleep, one arm bent over his head, shielding his eyes from the glow of the bedside light. So much for the new nightclothes, she thought as she pulled the duvet over her.

Roger Pender gazed at the blank television screen. Autumn was in the air and the room felt chilly. He got up to close the window wondering what it was that had puzzled him about the car the woman who had called herself Jane Stevenson had hired. He had sat behind the wheel and felt something was wrong. What had he taken in subconsciously? What had his brain registered but was failing to recall?

She had filled the tank with petrol, as instructed, as everyone did, or else they got charged for the fuel. The cars went out full and were returned in the same way.

Saffron Walden, she had said. She was going to visit her mother in Saffron Walden. From the bookshelf he took down his road atlas. Rickenham Green to Saffron Walden. A round trip of approximately 150 miles. Possibly a little more. Jane Stevenson or whoever she was had driven no more than sixty. But so what? Of course she had lied. She had lied about everything else and had made up the story about her mother. Was it worth telling the police? I suppose it's my duty to do so, he thought. But it could wait until the morning. He was weary and disappointed and wished he'd never met her.

In the bathroom he cleaned his teeth and noticed a few strands of grey in his thick brown hair. Let's face it, he thought, you just don't have any luck with women. Still, if he hadn't been interested in her and made the effort to ring her, the police wouldn't have made the connection between the stolen handbag and the hired car. Couldn't have, really, he thought, because they would have known nothing about it. He had met the real Jane Stevenson but he could not picture the woman who had used her name as a murderer. No, he decided, definitely not. He smiled at his reflection. Maybe, one day, when all this was over, he'd meet her again by chance.

15

It was raining. When John Short opened his eyes on Friday morning he could hear it drumming on the corrugated roof of the dustbin shelter beneath his window. The bedroom smelled stale, of sweat and alcohol, the fumes of which he had breathed out in the night. Brenda had refused his offer of a drink, as had Alan and Eddie. He had gone to the pub anyway. Brenda had Andrew, Eddie had a wife and children. But what on earth did Alan Campbell do with himself in the evenings? Short wondered. Cooked for himself, probably, because he was always stuffing his face, and then sat glued to the large TV set that took up half the space in his living-room. Strange bloke, lost interest in women after his wife left.

He opened the window and shivered. It wasn't cold, not yet, barely chilly really, it was only the shock of a drop in the temperature after the heatwave.

He went downstairs. His mouth was dry. Tea would be welcome. 'Oh, God.' In the kitchen, foil containers lay on the work-top, sauce from the curry staining it orange. What was left on the plate was congealed. At least, he thought, I used a plate. He didn't always. He filled the kettle.

Sticking through his letter-box were the daily paper and the *Rickenham Herald*. Rolled together they formed a thick wodge of paper which forced the letter-box wide open. Short retrieved them and went back to the kitchen to make tea.

He sat at the small formica table dressed in underpants and a T-shirt, his night-time attire, and read the front page of the *Herald*. The usual stuff about the body of a man, suspicious death, police asking for witnesses, blue car, blah, blah, blah. But what else could the Superintendent have given them? The truth? The bloody awful shocking facts? No way, José

Someone he knows, he thought. It has to be someone he knows. Someone we know, too, or have at least spoken to. But who? Short looked at his watch in which he also slept. It was early yet, plenty of time for more tea, plenty of time to rehydrate. While the kettle boiled again he scooped up the empty containers and threw them in the nearly full pedal-bin along with others which had held Chinese food. The only time he ate properly was when he took Nancy out for a meal. She expected the best and he provided it. He had nothing else upon which to spend his money. The house, bought years ago when prices were low, was paid for now. Clothes did not interest him, neither did cars or gadgets. His only real interest, apart from women, he realised, was crime and the solving thereof.

Perhaps the Chief would agree to let him off the rest of those damn interviews and allow him to study the statements. Accepted, Alan Campbell never missed a link, no matter how tenuous, but that was only because he was computer literate, he could make a machine do his thinking for him. What Alan doesn't have, and never will have, is a sense of something not being quite right – all right then, a gut feeling, if you're into police jargon, he thought.

The rain was heavier now. It pattered against the grimy window and snaked its way down to the rotten woodwork of the outside windowsill. 'Shit.' Short got up and rolled up a tea towel which he placed along the bottom of the frame where, if it continued to rain, water would seep in. The tea towel would probably be soaked when he got back later. If he had a wife she could see to things like that, get men in to do the necessary repairs. He had neither the time nor the inclination to do so himself and did not know one end of a hammer from the other. But he didn't want a wife, life was perfect just as it was.

Imagine not being able to stay in the pub as long as I like, to come home as and when I please, take off my shoes, slump in a chair with a beer and a take-away and watch one of the numerous channels I find myself in possession of these days. Alan Campbell had talked him into getting satellite television. God knows why, it was the same old rubbish no matter how much choice there was. It was a good job he liked rubbish. So this place is a tip. I like it that way.

Malcolm Graham had not liked it that way. His house had been neat and clean and tidy; a place for everything, everything in its place, as Short's mother used to repeat endlessly which was probably the cause for his sloppiness in adulthood. Until we marched in and did our stuff, he thought.

John Short knew his faults. He could never be faithful and had no intention of trying, therefore he would never marry, but it would not have crossed his mind to photograph young girls. It was women, real women, that interested him, and he did not expect any fancy stuff. Simple, straightforward, face-to-face sex, forget the frills.

It was a bit early in the day to be thinking like that but Short knew there had to be a reason for it. He wanted to go through those statements again. They had missed something, of that he was certain. Brutal; disgusting habits in the bedroom; egocentric – just a few of the characteristics ascribed to Graham. Enough there alone for someone to wish him dead . . .

'Last in again, I see,' Brenda commented a while later without a trace of malice or surprise. She was merely stating a well-known fact.

'Can't understand it. I've been up since the crack of dawn.' John was always late, renowned for his unpunctuality. It did not matter whether he allowed himself ten minutes or two hours, something always prevented him from being on time. Today it had been a dishcloth and lemon-scented liquid cleanser as he had attempted, unsuccessfully, to remove the latest stains from the kitchen surfaces. He'd have binned the shirt he had been wearing if the delicious detective Gibbons had not told him that ordinary toothpaste rubbed into curry stains would remove them once they went into the washing-machine. Women were amazing creatures.

The phone on Eddie's desk was ringing. Dressed casually but smartly, clean-shaven and smelling of shower-gel, Eddie went to anwer it. 'Yes, it is. Good morning, Mr Pender.' He reached for a pen, held the phone between ear and shoulder, not such an easy accomplishment with the modern slim receivers, and began to write. 'Thank you. We'll look into it right away.' He turned to face the others but the optimism in his voice was not matched by his expression. 'That was Pender. He said the woman posing as Jane Stevenson told him she was going to Saffron Walden to visit her mother. He says it was impossible because the mileage on the car was way out. She'd only driven fifty-nine miles.'

As one they turned to the second map on the wall of the

incident room, the one which covered the whole Division. Alan Campbell picked up a compass and calculated an area of thirty miles radiating out from Rickenham Green. 'It doesn't mean she drove twenty nine and a half miles one way and then back. She mightn't have left Rickenham at all,' he said. 'But at least we can chart the limits.'

Short was doodling on a piece of paper. 'But she could've driven seventeen miles to Saxborough, made the call to Graham from the phone box, driven seventeen miles back then five out to Frampton, five back, maybe more if she came by the longer route, and pottered around the lanes on Sunday morning to make it look worthwhile for her to have hired it at all. But so what? Until we know who she is it doesn't matter.' And the car had been clean, too clean. Forensics thought she may have put it through a car-wash herself before returning it. And then it had been cleaned professionally. There was no mud around the wheels, nothing to indicate it had ever been parked in a gateway.

'Supposing she didn't drive it at all, other than away from and back to the garage?' Eddie suggested. 'What if someone paid her to hire it, the same person who stole the handbag and was able to provide her with a false identity? Maybe the older woman Mrs Stevenson recalled seeing alone in the bar of the Coach and Horses? Of course, we don't know that a man didn't nick the bag.'

Ian was sitting in front of a desk, his head in his hands. 'There are far too many possibilities. We've got to narrow it down. We've got to concentrate on one thing at a time. For Christ's sake, we don't even know if the car hired from Roger Pender has anything to do with the murder.'

Short was poking around in his ear, one of his many habits which did little to endear him to his colleagues. 'If you ask me, we don't know bugger all about anything, apart from the fact that we've got a stiff who may simply have decided to top himself in one of the more unusual manners.' Nothing ever phased him, only twice in his life had he lost his temper. Inspector John Short could find amusement in any situation. He liked himself and he liked his life and could not understand those who did not. When he'd finished digging around in his ear he looked up and found four pairs of hostile eyes directed at him. 'Well, nothing's impossible.' But his mind was elsewhere. Going to Saffron Walden to see her mother. To see my mother. The words rang a bell. I wonder. He reached for the phone. 'Get me Mrs Jane Stevenson, please. She'll be at the DHSS offices.' He waited to be put through. 'Just thought I'd check. See where the real Mrs Stevenson's mother lives,' he said to no one in particular. 'Yes, hello. Sorry to bother you at work, but this might be important.' He asked the question and nodded. 'Is your mother's address or phone number in your diary? Okay. Thank you. We'll be in touch.' He replaced the receiver and grinned. 'We've just got lucky. I'll give you three guesses where Jane Stevenson's mother resides. Two words. Saffron Walden. But that information was not in Jane's handbag.'

Ian closed his eyes. This was it, this was the break they'd been waiting for. One slip of the tongue, one phone call had led them here. It was Brenda who expressed what they now knew had to be true. 'Then whoever took that handbag knows Jane Stevenson.'

'My mother's lived at the same address all her life. I was born there. I don't need to write it down in my diary to remember it,' she had explained to Short.

'What about the Brockham staff, the ones with children, do we carry on?' Alan asked.

'Yes. You, Eddie and Brenda try and get through the rest of them. I'll go and see Mrs Stevenson.' Ian paused and looked at Short who was rolling a pen on the desk. 'Want to go over the statements?' he asked. His reward was a large beam which creased the Inspector's face, causing half his moustache to disappear under plump cheeks and his eyes to vanish beneath bushy brows.

Left to his own devices, Short assembled all the files. 'Went to her mother's, a likely story,' he muttered as he started to read. Ten minutes later a memory stirred.

He pulled out Sheila Foster's file. 'I wonder.' Maybe sitting behind a desk wasn't such a good idea after all. He shuffled out of the incident room. 'I'll be in Ipswich if anyone wants me,' he called over his shoulder to the uniformed constable who was there to man the phones. 'I don't suppose they will, though,' he added to himself.

Jane hung up and explained to the supervisor that the police needed to speak to her. Another member of staff was sent to take her place behind the window at the counter. She and the Chief Inspector were given a small airless room in which to conduct the interview.

'What did Inspector Short mean, about wanting to know where my mother lives? She's not in any danger, is she?'

'No,' Ian answered, although he could not be sure. 'The thing is, if her address wasn't in the diary you keep in your handbag, how did this person know it? Whoever used your driving licence on Friday told Roger Pender that she was going to visit her mother in Saffron Walden. Would there have been a letter from her?'

Jane's naturally ruddy skin paled. 'I'll take time off work, go and stay with her. She's frail now, if anything happens, I'll never forgive myself. Oh, God, this is all my fault. If I hadn't started going to the pub –'

'Mrs Stevenson, please, don't.' Ian reached across the small battered table and patted her hand. 'You really mustn't think like that. She might have picked the name out of the air. Are you sure there wasn't anything to identify the place?'

'Quite sure.' Jane blew her nose on a tissue and sighed. 'No. That would be too much of a coincidence. Her guessing. It's someone I've spoken to. I suppose you want a list of everyone who knows me.'

'Yes. I do. And as soon as possible. Will they allow you some leeway here?'

'Yes. They know it's to do with Mr Graham. They can hardly refuse. Shall I do it now?' She reached for her handbag, the same one that was stolen, which now hung over the back of the chair in which she was seated. 'I've got my address book with me today.' She handed it to Ian. 'Everyone's in there. Oh, apart from George, of course.'

'I'll make sure this is returned to you by the end of the day. Do you think they'd let us have some tea?'

Jane smiled. 'It's all we survive on here. That and paracetamol. I'll get it. There's an urn in the kitchen, I won't be a minute.'

While she was gone Ian read the names written in Jane's neat hand. None of them were ones they had come across so far. Writing. There was another thing. The handwriting experts were agreed that the letters sent to Carmen Brockham and to Malcolm Graham had been written by different people. Maybe Sylvie Harris was telling the truth.

The tea was in plastic containers, white ones with ridges around the sides, the type that heat makes pliable so when you pick them up the pressure of finger and thumb guarantees that the contents slop over the top and burn you. Ian left his on the table to cool. 'What can you tell me about any of these people?' He indicated the address book. 'Anything different in their circumstances lately?'

'No. None that I know of. They're friends. Mostly people I've known a long time. A couple are tradesmen, the doctor, dentist, that sort of thing. Look, if any of them had been in the pub I'd have seen them.'

'What about the staff here? Do you socialise with any of them?'

Jane sighed and ran a hand through her hair. It had once been ginger, the cause of teasing at school, but was now a nondescript shade although still plentiful and naturally wavy; the overhead light in the unwindowed room caught at the few remaining gold strands. Ian imagined how she must feel, knowing all her friends to be under suspicion. 'No. I try to keep work separate. I go to the usual functions we hold, the Christmas party, the summer boat trip and the odd birthday drink, mostly without George. Since his back trouble we hardly go out at all.' She smiled again, showing small even teeth. 'One good thing. He's going to help Roger out a couple of mornings a week. Just putting the cars through the washer, light work, stuff he can handle. But he's like a different person already and he's only been there once.'

'Whose idea was that?'

'George's. Why?'

A whole new scenario flashed through Ian's mind. George had found out Jane stopped for a drink on the way home from work. He had gone to the Coach and Horses and taken her bag. Easy enough for him to have replaced it on the door handle. He had given someone her documents, told them to hire the car and bring it to him. He had then killed Malcolm Graham because . . . because what? His wife had been one of those young girls? She had had an affair with Graham because her husband was almost an invalid? Graham had tried to blackmail her and she had

139

confessed to her husband? It was possible. And now George was working at the garage. To keep an eye on things, to be on hand if the police started nosing around again? He could still drive, he could have got himself to Frampton.

'Chief Inspector?'

Jane was looking at him, her head on one side. 'I'm sorry. I was thinking about something. You were saying?'

'I asked why it was important, whose idea it was about George starting at Pender's.'

That could wait. 'No reason. I was sidetracked. Okay. Who else would know where your mother lives?'

'The fact that she lives in Saffron Walden is no secret. Even though I don't spend my free time with the people I work with, I get on well with most of them. We chat. Anyone here might know it.'

Ian stood. He'd be glad to leave the stuffy room. 'I hope I haven't taken up too much of your time. As I said, I'll make sure you have this back today.' He waved the address book in front of her then put it in his jacket pocket. 'If you can think of anyone else who might know, give me a ring on this number.' He handed her a card.

'There's something . . . No, sorry – it's gone again.' She shook her head.

'Anything might be useful.' Ian was on his feet, ready to leave.

'I don't know. I keep thinking there's something I ought to remember. Someone I did tell once. It just won't come back to me.'

'Well, it might come back to you if you try to forget it. It often works for me. If you do remember, please ring me.'

'I will.'

Ian left the building and stepped outside into the coolness of rain. No shower this time but proper rain, a steady hissing from a uniform grey sky. He turned up his collar and ran for the car. Once inside it, he reached under the dashboard and found a packet of cigarettes. He lit up, inhaled deeply and blew smoke out of the open window. This time he had gone almost a week. His longest period of abstinence had been three months and there had not been a second when the craving had receded or when Moira and his colleagues had not suffered. He was, he knew, becoming cantankerous. The more petty restrictions the government tried to impose, the more they tried to quash any enjoyment, the more he rebelled. And then he felt guilty, aware of his health. Children as young as six and seven were suffering from stress because of their forced awareness of famine and poverty, drugs and AIDS, the dangers of smoking and drinking and, more and more, eating. 'If we're all going to die anyway, and sooner than intended listening to some of the scare-mongers, then why can't they let us go to the devil our own way?' Ian said aloud. He grinned. A passer-by had bent her head to witness him talking to himself. 'It's probably CJD,' he called to her from the open window as she hurried away without looking back.

He had smoked a second cigarette by the time he returned to the station and felt a great deal better for it.

'Bloody weather.' Scruffy Short was in a line of traffic on the A12, his speed inhibited by the lack of visibility because of the spray from lorries. Yet he knew he'd be the first to complain if every-one was zipping along at seventy or more in such conditions. Unlike the Chief, he had no qualms about his lifestyle. Not for him the misery of even temporary abstinence. It was doubtful a piece of fruit had ever seen the inside of his house and if there was a paunch he had not only earned it, but enjoyed earning it. And Nancy didn't seem to mind. He knew people who jogged or exercised, half starved themselves and ate food they couldn't possibly enjoy and, heaven help them, knew nothing of the delights of an evening in the pub. 'You can tell 'em a mile away,' he said to himself. 'Hangdog expressions, afraid of germs, afraid of everything. Their number'll be up one day anyway.' He wondered anew why he was thinking like this, why, several times during this investigation, the collective thoughts of the team had turned to excesses, to a certain way of living or not living.

It could be, he thought, that it wasn't only Malcolm Graham who had an obsession, an obsession linked with either greed or power. Power, most likely, as he had no need of money. Two of a kind, that's what it is. Whoever killed him also had an obsession, some driving force that led them to leave him dead and in that unspeakable condition.

Stuck behind a lorry, he thought of the women they had interviewed. His theory seemed valid. Carmen Brockham, in love for the first time, desperate to keep her man and for him to keep his job, how would she feel when her one chance of happpiness looked like disappearing? Sylvie Harris, likewise. Couldn't have the man, went after the job. Couldn't have that either so – no, it didn't ring true. Why would she chop off his dick? Hell hath no fury like a woman scorned? Nah, too obvious.

His cigarettes were out of reach. He found some chewing gum and stuck two strips in his mouth. He was on the outskirts of Ipswich. Finding a lay-by, he consulted a map. Good. Mrs Sheila Foster, widow, lived this side of the city. Short had no idea how old she was. If she hadn't reached retirement age she might be out at work. If so, he'd wait until she came home.

Sheila Foster did not work, had not done so for four years, not since her first-born grandchild had become ill. Her daughter had needed her far more than her employers had done. And there were two more grandchildren to think about. She wanted to spend time with them, and, when Inspector Short rang her doorbell, she was doing just that. Marion's children were with her until Sunday.

16

It was Friday and George would not be at Pender's Garage that day. It was his gloomy expression, the same way he had looked on those hospital visits, which had resurrected the memory. Hospitals and the woman in Brockham's. Elaine Pritchard. Had Elaine's daughter died? Was that why she was able to go out to work? Or had she been cured? 'Did I tell you who I saw working in Brockham's? Elaine Pritchard. That woman we used to see at the hospital with her daughter. The girl looked dreadfully ill. Do you remember them, George?'

George was standing by the sink, in Jane's way as she tried to make breakfast. She said nothing, the greyness of his skin told her he was genuinely in pain.

'I won't be going far today,' he said, nodding towards the window and the rain falling from a sky as grey as his face. 'Elaine Pritchard? Yes, I vaguely recall her. What was wrong with her daughter?'

'She didn't actually say. She was terribly thin – the girl, that is. She must've been about about fifteen or sixteen. Do you suppose she's dead?'

George smiled. 'Meet my wife, Jane, the eternal pessimist. It could be that she's recovered and gone off to university or got herself married.'

'I hope you're right. I haven't got time to eat this toast. You have it if you like. I must go or I'll be late. Anything you need in town?'

'No, I don't think so. If the weather should clear up I might go in to the library. See you later. Drive carefully.' I might even see if Roger fancies a pint at lunchtime, he thought. Roger Pender walked to work and it was Dean who took customers on test drives if they required one, so there wouldn't be a problem. He kissed Jane's face and waved from the window as she fastened her seat-belt.

It was the routine of married life, Jane thought as she waved back before joining the traffic heading towards the town centre. Getting up, showering, breakfast, desultory conversation then work. There were many occasions when she thought George wasn't listening to her. She would ask a question and by way of reply would receive a *non sequitur*. It might be two sentences later that George would answer her question, proving that he had been listening after all. Perhaps it's the pain, she thought, perhaps it takes a while for what I say to get through to him when he's suffering.

The underground car-park was almost full, as it always was on wet days. She hurried up to street level and into the building. Now she knew where Elaine worked she would make contact with her again. She had enjoyed speaking to her the few times they had met, despite the grim circumstances. No wonder she was looking at me like that, Jane realised as she got out the forms necessary for the day's work, it must've brought back memories.

Perhaps I'll pop in and see if she's there at lunchtime. I'd like to know what happened.

Before she could give the matter further thought her supervisor came to say that the police were on the phone and wanted to speak to her.

By the time Detective Chief Inspector Roper had left, taking her address book with him, she had forgotten all about Elaine Pritchard and Brockham's. All she could think about was that it might be someone she knew who had taken her handbag and hired that car. And that, somehow or other, her mother had been brought into it.

'Can I help you?' The woman who answered the door was big-boned and big-breasted but in proportion: a fifties-style pin-up, Short decided. Just the way he liked them. And she certainly didn't look old enough to be the mother of the woman they had interviewed; far from it. Despite the weather she was dressed in cream pedal-pushers, canvas shoes and a blue checked shirt. Her hair was still dark and held back in a barrette. Knocking on for sixty if her daughter was in her late thirties, but I still wouldn't say no, Short decided, wondering what sort of stunner she had been in her youth. Elaine Pritchard would probably take after her. There was a lot of truth in the saying about looking at the mother before you married the daughter. However, he had no intention of marrying and he was not there to socialise.

'Inspector Short. CID. Rickenham Green Division,' he said with a smile, producing his identity. Mrs Foster did no more than lower her eyes for a second. Like most people, she did not take the trouble to check it.

'Is anything wrong?'

'No. Just a few more questions, I'm afraid. May I come in?'

'Yes, of course. My grandchildren are staying with me. If you'll excuse me a minute, I'll tell them they can watch television while we talk.' She smiled. 'You've done them a favour. At their mother's insistence, their viewing time's restricted. Still, they've been stuck in the house for most of the day because of the weather. Please, take a seat.' She pushed open the door of the lounge then walked down the hallway towards the back of the house.

John Short whistled through his teeth. The house was terraced and from the outside could have been in any suburb in any town or city, but the inside had been transformed. The downstairs front and back rooms had been knocked into one. The floor was of honey-coloured polished wood, adorned by several gay rag rugs. The settee and matching armchairs had pale wooden arms and legs and were upholstered in tan and beige stripes; Swedish, he guessed. One of the long walls was made of stone with a huge open fireplace in its centre, two walls were white and the third, leading to the medium-sized garden at the back, was made entirely from glass. Tasteful, he decided as he tried to calculate how much it would have cost. You could tell a lot about a person from the surroundings they chose for themselves. Classy, was Sheila Foster. But he had thought that anyway as soon as he had seen her. The daughter obviously took after her.

'They'll be all right for half an hour. Can I get you some tea?' Sheila asked, coming quietly into the room.

'No, thank you. I didn't realise you had grandchildren, Mrs Foster.'

'There was no reason why you should have done.' She sat down opposite him and crossed one slender leg over the other at the knee. 'Now, I can only presume you're here because of what happened to Elaine's boss. I can't think why, there's nothing to add to what I've already told the police.'

'I'm sure there isn't. It's just that I'd like you to go over last Saturday again. I'm not always the quickest on the uptake, I like to get things straight in my head.'

Sheila Foster pursed her lips but said nothing. She must be careful, the man was trying to trick her somehow. Her statement had been clear, concise and unambiguous. She had said or done nothing to arouse suspicion. She would humour him. 'What is it you'd like me to say? That I've suddenly remembered some vital piece of information, such as that my daughter arrived here dripping blood?' she asked with another smile.

'Why should there be any blood?' Got you, Short thought for a fleeting second. Whoever had spoken to Mrs Foster when they checked Elaine Pritchard's alibi would not have mentioned the manner of Malcolm Graham's death.

'Well, I imagined, as he'd been stabbed, there was bound to be

145

some, if not a lot. Stabbed more than once, from what the paper said.'

'You get the *Rickenham Herald* here?'

'No. Elaine told me. Anyway, if it pleases you, I'll repeat what I told the other officer.

'As I'm sure you already know, we were celebrating my birthday. Elaine had arranged to come over to see me. She had taken that Saturday off especially. My other daughter couldn't make it until later because an emergency had cropped up on her husband's side of the family. Elaine had been shopping, she had several carrier bags with her, one of which contained my present. As I don't have a garage she had to leave the car in the street so she brought the things in with her rather than tempt a thief.

'She'd also brought several bottles of wine which we started on straight away. Then she cooked me a lovely meal. We had some more to drink and I told Elaine that there was no way she could drive home. She agreed and said she'd love to stay the night. Marion stayed too, her husband babysat the children at home. Elaine left early in the morning but Marion stayed for the rest of the day. My neighbour can confirm that, they chatted for a while.'

'Can anyone confirm what time Elaine arrived?'

'I have no idea. I wasn't exactly expecting to be cross-examined about the events taking place on that particular day.'

'And she drove here?'

'Yes. She could have got here easily enough by rail but the train service back to Rickenham Green is almost non-existent on Sundays.'

'But I thought she hadn't intended to stay.'

Sheila smiled widely. 'She hadn't. But you don't know me or my daughter. When we get together we tend to celebrate. Deep down she'd have known she wouldn't be driving home on Saturday night.'

'What colour is her car?'

Sheila blinked. God, I can't remember, she thought. 'A sort of silvery colour. I don't know what they'd call it these days.' Yes, she could picture it now, although she had no idea of the make.

'And she parked outside?'

146

'No. Around the corner. There's never any room here at week-ends. It's as well I don't have a car myself,' she added before he could ask.

'I see. The grandchildren are your younger daughter's?'

'Yes. Inspector Short, why are you really here? If you had any doubts you'd only need to read my statement. I cannot think why you're so interested in Elaine's movements. For heaven's sake, she hardly knew the man, she'd only worked there for five or six months. We spent an innocent weekend together and that's all there is to it.'

'Why did your daughter and her husband divorce?'

'Really, this is going too far.'

Short didn't move. He arched his fingers and studied them. He would sit there until he got an answer or she dialled head-quarters and had him removed.

Sheila sighed. 'Why does anyone get divorced? They stayed together longer than most, sixteen years. They tried hard but the marriage wasn't working. It was as simple as that. And they're lucky, they've remained friends.'

'There was no one else involved, no admission of adultery, maybe at a previous stage in the marriage?' Graham, seeing Elaine in the store, might have recognised her from an earlier time, might have threatened to tell her husband if she didn't pay up. No. That idea wouldn't work. Elaine Pritchard's divorce had come through before she had started working at Brockham's. 'Sixteen years, but there are no children?'

'No. There are none.' Not now, she thought, not any longer. I have not lied. Poor, poor Anna. And poor Elaine.

'All right, Mrs Foster. I think that's all I need to know. Thank you for your time.'

She got up and went to the door with him, grateful when one of the children appeared to ask if he might have some orange juice. It was enough of a distraction because the Inspector seemed about to change his mind and ask more questions.

Back in the car John Short tugged at his moustache. What is she not saying? he asked himself. What is it she doesn't want me to know? And why did I feel the need to speak to her myself? Because the woman who hired the car said she was going to visit her mother and, whoever she was, she had stolen but then returned the handbag and was therefore, murderer or not, basically honest. Stick to the truth, it's easier, someone had once told him. Had that woman been Elaine Pritchard? Had she really been to visit her mother but at a later time than Mrs Foster would have them believe?

Clutching at straws, he thought. Up a creek without a paddle. I hope she doesn't make a complaint.

He depressed the clutch and began the journey back. Just you wait, my lovely, he thought. Nancy of the plump thighs and fiery hair had asked him for a date. He grinned. 'I've booked a table for two at the Duke of Clarence for nine thirty. You're paying,' was what she had actually said.

By mid-morning the rain had eased off enough for George to decide to go out. He'd go mad if he stayed in the house any longer. At eleven thirty he put on a raincoat and walked the mile and a quarter to the ugly modern red-brick library. It had blue-painted poles around the top of it and a diamond-shaped glass dome. Most people agreed with him when he said that it looked unfinished, as if someone had forgotten to remove all the scaffolding, rather than a commendable piece of architecture. He could have taken a bus but did not fancy being jerked around by one of the more heavy-handed drivers who made the vehicle lurch every time they changed gear. Besides, he had been told to exercise gently or his muscles would become even stiffer.

The usual library hush was broken by a group of three- to four-year-olds, seated on the floor cross-legged as one of the librarians read to them.

George went to the fiction section, chose two books there, then a biography. Was there something on the shelves marked 'Hobbies' worth browsing through, something he could learn easily and do at home as Jane had suggested? He spent fifteen minutes looking but the selection wasn't great, mostly knitting, sewing and cookery.

He was surprised to see it was almost twelve thirty as the computer scanned the spines of his books. Pender's Garage was no distance away. His back ached, but no longer unbearably so. He would call in and see if Roger was interested in that pint.

'I wasn't expecting to see you today, George. There's nothing for you to do, I'm afraid.'

'I don't think I'm up to it anyway. I was going to suggest a quick half in the Three Feathers. I don't suppose you frequent the Black Horse.'

'Not often.' The Black Horse was the nearest pub – like the garage it was in Saxborough Road. It was rough and noisy and not the place for a quiet conversation. 'The Feathers sounds fine to me. Dean, I'm going out. Shouldn't be more than forty-five minutes,' he called into the showroom as he shrugged his arms into a waterproof jacket.

The two men walked down the road, avoiding the water thrown up by the cars. They crossed by the bridge which spanned a tributary of the River Deben and made their way to the pub at the top of the High Street.

'I'll get them,' Roger said. 'What'll it be?'

'Guinness for me, please, Roger. Do you mind if we sit down?'

'We might as well while there's room. Fancy a sandwich or anything?'

'No, just a drink. Making myself a snack gives me something to do. You carry on if you're hungry. I'll find a table.' George looked around and chose a small one in the window beneath the false leaded panes and the threadbare velvet curtains. But it was still better than the Black Horse. The outing was doing him good. He must do things more often, even simple things like this if they lifted the depression which sometimes settled upon him when he was housebound or in pain.

Roger returned with the drinks. 'Have the police been back to you?'

'No. But Jane rang me just before I came out. They've been to see her again, at work this time.'

'Do they know anything?'

'Difficult to say. She was a bit upset. They've taken her address book with them. Apparently they were following up something you told them, something to do with this woman having a mother in Saffron Walden. Well, Jane's mother lives there, you see. It's too much of a coincidence for her to have made it up – at least, that's what they think. And this has led them to believe that whoever took Jane's bag knows her.'

'God, how awful. But did anyone you know know this Malcolm Graham?'

149

George shook his head and wiped froth from his mouth with a tissue. 'I've never heard anyone mention his name, but that doesn't mean they didn't. However, they still don't know if there's any connection between the two things. Oh, well, I suppose we'll just have to wait and see.' But Jane had mentioned Brockham's only that morning. Something about a woman called Elaine Pritchard working there. She would have known Malcolm Graham. And she knows us. Yes, he thought, I do remember her now. Striking-looking woman, sickly-looking daughter. How could he have forgotten?

He told Roger what Jane had told him, and about the connection he had just made and Jane's fears about the girl. 'I was in agony, I can tell you, but I must've noticed this Elaine anyway, because I can see her face now, even if I wasn't aware of it then. Perfect figure, big sad eyes and hair like you don't see very often on British women, really dark, almost black, natural, too.'

Roger's mouth went dry. The description fitted the woman who had walked into reception. Could this possibly be the same person? Yes, it could, even if she only knew the real Jane Stevenson a little. 'And she works at Brockham's, you say?'

'So Jane said. They sort of half recognised each other.'

'Which department?'

'Haven't got a clue. I know we bought perfume for the daughter-in-law's birthday because Jane gave me the receipt. I had to give her some money. She'd got her credit cards back with the handbag but we'd already cancelled them and the new ones hadn't come through then. Jane's dead straight with money. She'd spent a bit more than we'd bargained for and was worried I'd be annoyed otherwise I'd have forgotten what she bought. Birthdays and Christmas are her department. Anyway, can I get you another?'

'Just a half.' Roger wanted to leave immediately but it would be rude and he needed time to think, to assimilate what George had told him and work out what to do about it. He hardly joined in the conversation which followed but tried to make it seem as if he was interested.

'No thanks, George, not today. I have to get back. Can you come in on Monday? We get a lot of cars back after the weekend,' he said when his glass was empty and George offered to refill it.

150

'I'd be glad to. See you then. Have a good weekend.' George remained where he was. He would have one more drink then go home. By the time he walked back, had something to eat and cleared up there would not be long until Jane came home. Sitting there, in solitude but not alone, he saw where the attraction of the half-hour in the pub had lain for his wife. Yes, thirty minutes when no one could make demands of her was the least she deserved.

Roger walked quickly back to the garage. He wanted to act immediately but Dean was not only entitled to a break, he had a dental appointment. It would be today. 'Go on, push off for an hour,' he said.

Trade began to pick up as those who had managed to leave work at lunchtime came in to collect pre-booked cars or hire one at the last minute. A problem arose with one of the vehicles. For no apparent reason it refused to start. 'Damn the thing,' Roger swore, knowing there was nothing of similar size and power he could offer his client. After several telephone calls one of his rivals agreed to drive over with a similar model as long as someone could drive him back again. It would have to be Dean. Roger was probably still under the limit but he'd had a couple of drinks the previous night and could not take the chance. Having a drink/driving offence would hardly attract business.

Dean had said he didn't mind staying on until seven but two latecomers kept Roger until after five thirty. By the time the paperwork was complete there was not time to get to Brockham's before it closed at six.

Back in his flat he paced the floor. He was meeting some friends for dinner. Ought he to ring the police? No. How ridiculous he would look. He had never set eyes on Elaine Pritchard and it would cause great embarrassment to her, especially as she had been employed by the murdered man. Besides, she would naturally be looking sad if her daughter was so ill. He would leave it until the morning and try to enjoy himself.

When Jane got back from work that evening George was looking through the classified pages of the *Rickenham Herald*. 'You're serious, then, about moving?' she asked as she looked over his shoulder.

'Only if you're in agreement. You were right, what you said, about me needing something to do. A garden would provide an answer.' He reached for her hand. 'What do you say?'

'Yes. Let's do it.'

'It makes such a difference, you see, love. For instance, today.' George told her of his outing and his drink with Roger Pender. 'Small things, maybe, but it made me see where I was heading if I continued to stay at home moping.

'I mentioned that woman you were talking about. Elaine Pritchard. Don't ask me how we got around to that. Roger seemed a bit funny about it, he went rather quiet. I wonder if he knows her and I said something out of place. Jane? What is it?' She was staring at him, an expression of horror on her face.

'George, I've just remembered. I knew something was bothering me when that Chief Inspector came to see me at the office. I told her where I went after work. When you were in with the specialist we were discussing ways of coping. I'm sorry, perhaps I shouldn't have confided in a stranger, but it wasn't easy when you were at your worst. You see, she knew I had a drink at the Coach and Horses every day.' She paused. 'And I also told her where my mother lived. What shall I do? I mean, do you think the police ought to know?'

'You didn't see her in the pub, did you?'

'No. But it just seems to fit somehow. It seems so awful because I liked her, I know she would be the sort of person to return my handbag. But why on earth did she take it in the first place? Why did she want to hire a car secretly? As far as I'm aware she doesn't have a husband to hide things from. They were going through a divorce when I first met her.'

'Look, we don't know it was her. It could have been a stranger who saw an opportunity and took it. Don't make trouble for her, not when she's got enough on her plate.'

'But she works at Brockham's, George, think about it. It all fits together somehow.'

George nodded. 'Go on, then, ring the man who spoke to you this morning. If she's innocent I suppose it can't do any harm.'

It was Brenda Gibbons who took the call because Ian had already gone home.

Jane Stevenson passed on the information and hung up. What she had omitted to say was that Elaine Pritchard had been at the hospital because her daughter needed treatment.

17

'I'm off out of it,' Short announced. He stood up and brushed crumbs from his lapel. He had eaten a biscuit with his mug of tea. There was always a packet of chocolate digestives amongst the muddle his desk drawer contained.

'But what are we going to do about Elaine Pritchard?' Brenda looked away, wishing she hadn't used the plural. Jane Stevenson had just telephoned, she could deal with it herself. Why should Scruffy Short have the glory if there was anything in what Mrs Stevenson had told her? 'Forget it. I know you're going out.' It was already after six. Friday night and she was stuck at headquarters. Andrew would be home very soon. They might both work in Rickenham Green but they needed two cars to get there. Neither of them worked particularly sociable hours and there never seemed to be enough time to spend with him. But how he spoiled her. It was hard to get used to going home to a meal he had prepared if he happened to arrive before her.

Shall I ring the Chief? she wondered as Short left in a cloud of body odour. How did his woman stand it? Brenda imagined sharing a bed with him and almost gagged. Hopefully he would shower before he went out.

She picked up the telephone receiver. Someone else in authority ought to know now that Short was no longer on the premises. It might as well be Ian Roper.

'Can you deal with it?'

'Yes, sir. I just wanted to check it was okay to go ahead and speak to her.'

'Can there be anything in it? She doesn't have any children and she's worked at Brockham's less than a year. Surely if there was anything between them in the past Graham wouldn't have taken her on. She certainly wouldn't have taken the job.' But, Ian was thinking, she may still be the person to have taken Jane Stevenson's handbag in order to hire a car. There was still nothing concrete to point to the two crimes being connected, only the sighting of a parked blue car near the scene.

Brenda verbally echoed his thoughts. 'It's hard to say. But it does seem to add up. The bag, the hired car, knowing where the mother lived and a Brockham's employee.'

'Is anyone else there?'

'I think Alan's still around somewhere.'

'Take him with you. If not, find someone who's free. Don't take any chances. If she was responsible for what happened to Malcolm Graham she could be very dangerous.'

'I will, sir. Have a good evening.' He had mentioned going to see something at the Rickenham Playhouse.

'Thank you.' And he would. He thought he deserved it. It felt as though Mark's wedding was in the distant past although it was less than a week ago. To appease Moira, of whom he had seen so little during the week, he had bought tickets for a new production of Harold Pinter's *The Birthday Party*. She had assured him he would enjoy it and that it would be nothing like some of the heavier stuff to which she had subjected him. 'Give my regards to Andrew.'

'I will.' Andrew. No hesitation that time. The Chief had not had to stop himself calling him the Ugly Brute. Things were looking up.

'Alan, we're to see Elaine Pritchard again. Can you come with me now?' she asked once she had found him.

He looked up from the computer, not in the least bothered that it was Friday night and the rest of their team had already gone home. 'Again?'

Brenda explained the reason why it was necessary. Alan made no comment but his face was grim.

The rain had stopped altogether. A rainbow arced over the buildings and sunshine lit the treetops as they drove to the small estate of bungalows where Elaine lived. The wooden gate stood wide open. Her car was in the drive, a silver one, just as Sheila Foster had told John Short. Alan pulled in behind it as there were double yellow lines marked on that side of the road.

The woman who answered the door was not Elaine Pritchard

but looked very much like her. She had a drink in her hand and the smell of cooking drifted down the hall. 'Is Elaine Pritchard at home?' Alan asked.

'Yes. Elaine?' Marion called over her shoulder.

Elaine appeared from a doorway. She stood still and inhaled deeply. It was a shock seeing the female detective who had spoken to her before. 'Come in,' she said, knowing she could not avoid talking to them. 'This is my sister, Marion Collins.'

'What's going on?' Marion asked, although she was in no doubt that their presence was connected with the death of her sister's employer.

'We'd like to talk to you alone, Mrs Pritchard, if that's all right with you?' Brenda said, noticing how pale she was, how much her hands trembled.

'Yes. Yes, of course.' Her voice was barely audible. 'Would you mind finishing off the meal for me?' she asked, turning to Marion.

'Of course not.'

'We'll go in here.' Elaine led them to an obsessively tidy living area, half lounge, half dining-room in open-plan style. She sat down but said nothing, waiting for one of them to speak first.

'Where were you last Friday evening?' For once Alan was taking the initiative.

'I've already told you, it was Mum's ... Oh.' She stopped. Friday, not Saturday. 'At work during the day. I came straight home and spent the evening alone.'

'We believe you know a Mrs Jane Stevenson.'

Elaine frowned. 'Yes. I met her at Rickenham General where Mr Stevenson was undergoing treatment. The husband had something wrong with his back. But I've never spoken to her except at the hospital, and the last time must've been at least a year ago. But she did come into the store very recently. I was really pleased to see her but we didn't get a chance to talk. Why are you asking me questions about her?'

'Because Mrs Stevenson had her handbag stolen while she was having a drink in the Coach and Horses last Friday evening. Later, it was returned to her.'

'I still don't understand. What has any of this to do with me?'

155

'You knew she went to that particular pub every day after work. She had told you as much.'

Brenda was surprised at the sternness in Alan's voice. Not only was he asking all the questions, he sounded authoritative. She hoped he was not about to punish this woman for the things his own wife had done to him.

'I can't say that I do remember her telling me. Besides, why should I take her handbag? None of this makes any sense to me.' She was twisting her hands in her lap and very close to panicking. 'I need a drink of water. Is it all right if I go and get one?'

Alan glanced at Brenda. She nodded. If Elaine Pritchard took off via the back door they would know she was guilty of something.

Marion stood by the cooker, a saucepan lid in her hand as she stared at the contents of the pan. 'Will they be much longer? This is almost ready.' She turned around. 'Elaine? For God's sake, what's the matter?' Moving quickly across the room she put her arms around her sister. Never had she seen her face so full of anguish, not even when Anna died. She pushed her gently into a chair and refilled the wineglass she had been using prior to the arrival of the police.

'I can't take any more. I just keep remembering Anna.'

'Stay there and don't move. I'll sort this out.' Marion walked swiftly into the living area and stood, her hands on her hips, in front of the two visitors. 'I don't know what you're playing at but you're being damn insensitive. Elaine's been through a hell of a lot. Apart from this place she's lost everything. First her husband, then her child. And to cap it all she's just gone through the first anniversary of Anna's death.'

A child? Brenda thought. A child that no one had heard of at Brockham's or elsewhere. Mrs Pritchard had certainly never mentioned one. One year. How many acts of revenge were committed on an anniversary? 'How old was Anna when she died?'

'Seventeen.'

'Mrs Collins, would you mind answering a few questions?'

'No. Not if it means Elaine doesn't have to suffer any more.'

Marion sank into an armchair, calmer now that she had said her piece.

'Was it Anna who needed hospital treatment?' Brenda took over.

'Yes.'

'What was wrong with her?'

'No one really knew for certain. From the time she was twelve she began acting oddly. When she was fourteen it was obvious she was psychologically disturbed. She almost stopped eating and then she started hurting herself. Self-harm, I think, is what they call it. Even her psychiatrist couldn't understand it. She had two loving, stable parents, she was doing well in school and there was no question of child abuse. It was just one of those things, something inherent in her that no one could have prevented. The loose diagnosis was schizophrenia but they were never very certain.

'When Anna was fifteen Elaine gave up work to look after her. She couldn't be left alone, you see, and there was no chance of her going back to school. She did it there, too, cut herself, it was upsetting the other kids. Elaine got a private tutor but in the end he gave up on her. She'd just stare out of the window. That's all she did really, stare at things or hurt herself. And then, when she was seventeen she killed herself.

'It was the most awful day of Elaine's life. The pressure had been building up. Brian, Elaine's husband, took as much time off work as he was able to, to provide some respite for Elaine, but in the end the strain of being constantly vigilant was too much for them both. They split up. I have to give Brian his due, he still did his share as far as Anna was concerned even after he'd left home.

'There was no chance of them getting back together. You see, Anna killed herself at a time when Brian was with her. Elaine admits she's in the wrong but she blamed him, she felt if she'd been here it wouldn't have happened. It would have, though. Maybe not that day, but it would've happened sooner or later.' She shrugged, a gesture of sadness. 'That's it really. Elaine went back to work, getting that job at Brockham's, and tried to pick up the pieces.'

157

'Did she ever mention Malcolm Graham before she went to Brockham's?'

'Not that I can recall. I mean, she's hardly mentioned him since she's been there.'

'So she wouldn't have known him prior to her taking the job?'

Marion's dark hair swung as she shook her head. 'Definitely not. She'd have said if she recognised him.'

'Thank you. You've been very helpful.'

'Is that it? Shall I tell Elaine you're leaving?'

'I need to make a telephone call first. Excuse me.' Alan went outside and used the car phone. If Roger Pender was available they'd ask him to come to the station to identify, or otherwise, Elaine Pritchard as the woman who had hired the car. If not, it could wait until the morning. There was no evidence to support the theory that Anna Pritchard's death was in any way involved with more recent events. With her sister, who came across as sensible and down-to-earth, on the premises it was unlikely that Mrs Pritchard would do a disappearing act.

But Roger Pender was not at home, or not answering the telephone. DC Alan Campbell left a message for him to ring them as soon as he possibly could.

When he returned Brenda stood up ready to accompany him. At long last she could go home and spend what was left of the evening with Andrew.

Marion was showing them to the door when Elaine came into the hall. She was steadier now, in control. 'I take it you won't need to speak to me again?'

'Of course they won't,' Marion told her. 'They can see how upsetting this has been for you. Goodnight.' Marion was closing the door before they were properly through it.

'A seventeen-year-old daughter. What do you make of that?'

Alan shook his head. 'Not a lot, not if she'd been ill all that time. And look at it this way, if Mrs Pritchard was making trips to the hospital, worried sick about her daughter, she'd hardly be likely to be taking in inconsequential bits of chat while she waited to see the doctor. Anyway, we'll get her and Roger Pender in in the morning and see if they know one another.'

Brenda felt they should be doing something more but there

158

was a limit on the amount of hours they could work competently during a day. Home, she thought, and Andrew.

'I told you you'd enjoy the play,' Moira said as she got out the sandwiches she had prepared in advance for supper. 'Want a beer?'

'Why not indeed? I'm just going to make a call first.' In the hall where the telephone sat on a half-moon table, he dialled the number for the incident room and spoke to the officer on duty. 'How did Brenda and Alan get on with the Pritchard woman?' Ian listened to the outcome of the interview. A daughter. A disturbed daughter at that, one who had eventually killed herself. And why had the woman never mentioned her? 'Okay, I want you to find out the name of Anna Pritchard's specialist at Rickenham General. Yes, I know what they're like about digging out admin staff at night but I need the information by the morning. When you get hold of the psychiatrist, if you get hold of him, tell him we need to know when treatment started and why, and, in his opinion, why she killed herself.'

'I heard what you said. Who's Anna Pritchard?' Moira placed a glass of beer and a plate in front of Ian. He reached for a sandwich.

'She's the daughter of one of the staff at Brockham's. Or was. But for some reason Mrs Pritchard has been keeping her existence a secret.'

'I expect if she went back to work to start a new life she wouldn't want everyone feeling sorry for her. And some people still think there's a stigma attached to both mental illness and suicide. I'm sure I wouldn't want everyone discussing it. Oh, I see.' Moira realised why it might be important. Anna Pritchard might have been one of Malcolm Graham's victims. In which case her mother would have two reasons for wanting him dead; for what he had done to Anna and had caused Anna to do to herself.

Ian had relaxed during the play. They had had drinks during the interval and he had offered to buy her chocolates which she never ate and had therefore refused. But the gesture had been appreciated. To talk of work any longer would ruin any benefit he had gained from the evening. Moira decided it was time to change the subject.

18

One week to the day of the murder, Ian thought as he drove in to work. It was early, a little after seven thirty, and the Saturday streets were quiet. No one much about except roadsweepers, milkmen, postmen and policemen. The information he had requested was waiting for him. Friday night or not, someone at Rickenham General hospital had found the relevant file and got in touch with Dr Freeman who would, if he kept to his word, be arriving at headquarters at eight o'clock.

'No problem,' he had told the officer who had contacted him. 'I'm playing golf at nine. I'll call in on my way to the Elms.'

A car Ian did not recognise was parked near his own space. A set of golf clubs sat on the back seat. Ian shook his head. Probably all right in a police station car-park, but the good doctor ought to take more care elsewhere and lock them in the boot.

James Freeman was fresh-faced and boyish-looking and showed none of the strain usually associated with his profession. Must be the exercise of walking the course, Ian decided as he shook the man's hand before taking him up to his office.

'You wanted to know about Anna Pritchard,' Freeman began. He placed a folder on Ian's desk. 'It's all in here, case notes, et cetera, but I suspect I can remember most of the things you'll want to ask me.

'In case you were wondering, it was suicide, Chief Inspector. There's no question of that. It was always on the cards, even her parents accepted that.'

'Always?'

'I meant over the last couple of years. Before that she was showing an improvement.'

'When did her problems start?'

'She was about twelve when her mother noticed changes in her, nothing too obvious at first. At thirteen she started eating less, Mrs Pritchard naturally assumed she was becoming anorectic and took her straight to her GP. The GP fortunately realised the problem was even more complex than that, and he referred her to me as an out-patient. Apart from not eating she had started cutting herself.

'She was fifteen by the time we had her stabilised and I began to hope for better things. Then, suddenly, her condition deteriorated rapidly. Anna's parents had to watch her every minute. We had her in, of course, but that didn't work and I had to accept that she was a little better when she was at home so we discharged her.'

'What caused the deterioration?'

'We were never certain. There was no doubt that many of her actions were attention-seeking. At one point she claimed she'd been subjected to a sort of rape but Mrs Pritchard hadn't contacted the police and there seemed to be no evidence of this. I questioned her closely but she clammed up and refused to say any more. Then, as I say, she took her own life. Her father found her in the bath, her wrists cut. She'd done a good job, this was no cry for help. I suspect she knew her father wouldn't go in to check on her as her mother would have done. No one knew where she concealed the knife. It was a knife. There were never any razor blades about.

'He called an ambulance and got her to hospital, but it was too late. May I ask why you need to know her history?'

'Dr Freeman, I think there's a chance Anna was telling the truth, I think she may well have been raped or sexually abused in some way. If I showed you some photographs would you be able to pick her out?'

'Yes.'

Ian emptied an envelope on to the table and spread out the pictures. James Freeman studied them carefully then pointed to one of them. 'That's her. God, the poor thing.'

They both looked at the half-clothed young girl in her indignity. There was terror in her face. Ian had seen the picture before but it still sickened him.

'Thank you for coming in. I hope you're not late for your game.'

'My partner will wait, he likes playing against me.' He grinned. 'I'm the only person he can beat.'

Ian walked back to the main entrance with him and watched as he pushed open the glass door. When? he thought. When would there have been an opportunity for Malcolm Graham to get hold of the girl when she was under almost constant supervision?

'Sir?' The desk sergeant was trying to gain his attention. 'There's a call for you, shall I get them to put it through to your office?'

'Please.'

It was Roger Pender. He apologised for not ringing sooner but he had been out to dinner with friends and had stayed overnight. 'I've just got home,' he said. 'Is there any news on the woman who hired the car?'

'Possibly. Mr Pender, we'd like you to come in and confirm whether or not a certain lady is the one who came to you using Jane Stevenson's identity. We wondered whether you'd be prepared to do so this morning?'

'Yes. My assistant's opening up for me. Shall I come right away?'

'If it's convenient, we'd be very grateful. Thank you.' Ian went down to the general office. DCs Gibbons and Roberts were hunched over some files, John Short was staring out of the window. 'Pender's on his way in,' Ian told them. 'And the shrink happened to mention that Anna Pritchard claimed she was raped.'

'Raped? By Graham?' Short asked as he turned to face the room.

'We don't know. She refused to say. Okay, bring Elaine Pritchard in. Don't say anything other than we need to ask her a few more questions.'

The rain had ceased during the night and now the sky was blue. It was warm but not hot. Brenda, in pleated trousers and a plain T-shirt, stood and tightened the band holding back her hair. Eddie Roberts followed her out of the room.

'Are we ever going to get a replacement sergeant?' Short asked Ian. The one sergeant they had was on holiday and since the second, DS Markham, had been killed during the course of another case there had been no sign of anyone to take his place.

'Next week, the Super tells me. But he said that last week.

162

Someone by the name of Gregory Grant, can you believe? Sounds like a film star. Recently promoted, I understand, and new to the area. He's just had his appendix out.' And no sign of Scruffy Short being shunted elsewhere, he thought. Still, Ian was learning to live with him.

They sat in silence wondering if there was any truth in the rape story until someone rang to say that Mr Pender was downstairs. This is it, this has to be it, Ian thought as he went down to meet him.

'This might sound a bit odd, but we'd like you to sit here.' Ian indicated the chairs lining the walls in the reception area, deserted at that time of day. 'In a few minutes two of my officers will come in with a lady. If you do recognise her, say nothing, just sit there. All right?' This way was far easier and far quicker and cheaper than an identity parade.

They waited another ten minutes before Brenda and Eddie appeared, one either side of Elaine Pritchard. Ian made eye contact with Roger, inclined his head almost imperceptibly and held his breath. No one spoke, no one moved, apart from the three people coming in through the door. They continued on through the reception area and disappeared into the back of the building. Elaine had not even glanced towards the seat.

'Well?'

Roger Pender was staring at the empty space where they had been. 'I don't understand it,' he said. 'It isn't her, but whoever she is she looks very much like her.'

'You're sure? You're certain it isn't the same woman?'

'Positive. I'm sorry.'

Ian sighed. Everything had been in vain. They were no nearer a solution than at the beginning. 'Thank you for your time, Mr Pender. I'm sorry to have inconvenienced you on a Saturday.'

Roger, too, was sorry. He had been hoping to see her, hoping to learn that whatever she had done it wasn't too serious and that he still might have the chance to take her out.

Elaine had been taken to an interview room and left in the company of a WPC. 'Any luck?' Eddie Roberts asked when he and Brenda met Ian in the corridor.

'No. Pender's certain it wasn't her although he said she looks similar.'

'Similar?' Brenda was staring at Ian. 'He said similar?'

'Yes.'

'The sister?'

'Pardon?'

'Elaine's sister. She's staying with her. They look very much alike.'

'Where is she now?'

'At the bungalow. She tried to insist upon coming too, but we dissuaded her.'

'Then you know what to do. And get Roger Pender back again. And for God's sake apologise to him.'

Once more DCs Roberts and Gibbons left the building.

Ian sighed. 'Here we go,' he muttered as he went into the interview room.

Elaine Pritchard sat on one side of the table. She was lovely in a gamin sort of way but she exuded sadness. Neatly dressed in her Brockham's uniform she appeared quite calm. 'I'll be late for work,' she said. 'Can't this wait?'

'I'm afraid not, Mrs Pritchard.' Ian sat down. 'Why have you never mentioned your daughter Anna to anyone?'

'Because she was a part of my life that's over. A special part that's private.'

'We understand she had psychiatric problems and that she took her own life.'

Elaine met his eyes and nodded, swallowing hard to stop herself from crying. Did the man have no compassion, did he not know how hard it still was for her to talk about Anna?

'I know it's distressing for you but I have to ask this, was your daughter raped?'

'No. She came out with things like that sometimes. We tried not to take any notice because we didn't want to encourage her.'

'You're certain of this?'

'Of course I'm certain. I'm her mother, for God's sake.'

'And she was under constant supervision?'

'Yes.'

But Ian had noticed the slight hesitation. He leant back in his seat, the cue for Inspector Short to take over.

'How was that possible?'

'My husband, ex-husband, helped me out. He knew it was impossible for me to be with her every second of the day and

164

night. As much as I loved her it would have driven me mad in the end. My mother was marvellous with her, she'd take her shopping, things like that. She said it was always easier being a grandparent. It was such a relief, being able to relax but knowing Anna was in safe hands.'

'How about when she was at school?'

Elaine looked away. 'All right, that was different. Obviously we couldn't be with her there. She absconded several times, they couldn't cope with her and she was disruptive in class. The head teacher explained that she had no hope of passing any exams, that her concentration was so poor she retained very little. We arranged for private tuition at home, but it was a waste of time. All I could think about was that she had no future.'

'Mrs Pritchard,' Short interrupted gently. 'Tell us about the times she absconded.'

'Anna would walk out of school. The school would telephone me and I'd go looking for her. She was nearly always in the town centre, just sort of hanging around. When I found her she'd come home readily enough but she'd never say why she did it. Once she was missing for several hours. I rang the police but she turned up at home while I was on the phone, none the worse for wear.'

'And afterwards, after she left school, did she disappear then?'

'Only once.'

'What happened on that occasion?'

'Why are you asking me all these questions? What has Anna got to do with anything?'

Both Ian and Short were wondering the same thing. Were they putting this woman through an unnecessary ordeal? 'We need to know, Mrs Pritchard,' Ian said, 'because we strongly believe there was a sexual motive behind Mr Graham's death.'

Elaine's face paled beneath the tan. 'What makes you think that?'

'From evidence which I am not prepared to disclose.'

'I see. You think he raped Anna and I killed him as an act of revenge?'

'We have to look at it as a possibility, as I'm sure you understand.'

'I did not kill him. I didn't like the man, but I didn't kill him.'

'The time Anna went missing from home, what happened?'

'I was in the kitchen making tea. I called out to her that it was ready. There was no reply. She'd gone. Crept out without my noticing. She returned after a couple of hours. She was over fifteen by then, Chief Inspector. I felt I had to begin letting go a little. For months previously she'd been showing great signs of improvement. Her psychiatrist was really pleased with her. But after that day she relapsed. There was talk of sectioning her under the Mental Health Act.'

'And when she returned?'

'It was a cold day. She was shivering and very pale. I ran her a bath and supervised her. She was very quiet and refused to talk to me. I picked up her clothes.' She stopped suddenly and bent her head over the table, wiping away tears with the back of her hand. 'Oh, God, I didn't know what to do. Her knickers were missing.' She took a tissue from her handbag and blew her nose. Tears still ran from her eyes. A few minutes later she began to speak again.

'Later that night she began to talk. I didn't know if she was making it up but she said she had thrown them in a bin because they were dirty, because she was dirty, and that she didn't deserve to live.'

'Did you believe her?'

Elaine nodded. 'Yes, I did. It wasn't the first time I'd witnessed this sort of behaviour.'

'Was there any mention of a man, of someone who might've touched her?'

'No. Not ever. Not even a hint.'

'Was there anyone else she might have confided in?'

'No.'

The answer was too quick, too certain for it to have been true. 'Your sister, perhaps? Your mother, or a school friend?'

'She had no friends. And, no, not my sister. With two small children she couldn't have coped with Anna as well so she usually only saw her with me or my mother.'

'All right, we'll leave it there for the moment. However, I'm afraid we need to detain you a little longer.'

The two men left the room, Short behind Ian. 'It doesn't look good for her,' Ian said. But deep down he understood the woman, he knew how he would feel if a man like Malcolm Graham defiled his child, a child who was under age and who had mental problems. Elaine Pritchard had devoted her life to caring for her daughter, a daughter who might have been raped and who then killed herself. And no husband to fall back on because the strain had already destroyed the marriage, he reminded himself.

Malcolm Graham had been an evil man. He had been murdered and mutilated. Ian, usually so fair-minded, knew he was wrong to do so but he felt that the victim had deserved his fate.

Waiting for them downstairs were Roger Pender and Marion Collins. Roger had positively identified the woman who had hired the car as Elaine's sister.

Two hours later Sheila Foster stirred sugar into her tea, took a sip, then smiled. 'Shall I start at the beginning?' she said, looking from the stern face of the Chief Inspector to the more sympathetic one of Detective Constable Gibbons.

19

Moira sat at the kitchen table wondering how much longer Ian would be. She had been gardening and was dressed in frayed jeans and a yellow T-shirt. Unaware of the fading daylight she studied a prospectus she had picked up in the public library that morning. Having passed A level law she was trying to decide which course to enrol in when evening classes started again in September. That she would probably never use the qualifications was irrelevant. It kept her mind active and provided her with a way of meeting new people. She liked her job in the offices of a garage showroom, a garage which sold only new, expensive models and therefore was not in competition with Roger Pender's business, and she had no intention of leaving it.

'You'll strain your eyes,' Ian said, making her jump as he came through the back door. He crossed the room and flicked on the light.

Moira looked up at him and doubted if he had ever looked more drawn. The lines were etched deeply into his face and stubble showed on his chin. Saturday night and he had just returned from a seven thirty start. Beer was the first requisite, she decided, and a glass of wine for herself.

Ian sat down and picked up the prospectus although he made no pretence of reading it. 'We arrested a woman today, a woman who tried to put things right. I don't feel good about it, Moira. She murdered a man but, to be honest, I wouldn't have been upset to see her walk free.'

Moira placed their glasses on the table. Because Ian had left so early that morning she had assumed he would be home at a reasonable hour and had therefore planned a special meal. By the look of him he would not feel like eating for a while, not until he had relaxed. And he hadn't even mentioned missing the Norwich City match. They had won, she would give him the good news before he spoke. For speak he would. She was perfectly aware that he was about to tell her all that had happened.

'Did they? I'm glad,' he said. 'That's the best thing I've heard all day.' He took a sip of beer then held the glass between both hands, moving it around on the table where it left damp patches. 'The woman I told you about, the one whose daughter committed suicide. We thought it was her. The daughter was abused by Malcolm Graham when she was fifteen.'

'How awful. Did she understand what was happening to her?'

'Oh, yes. She wasn't subnormal or whatever the latest politically correct phrase is. She understood, all right. We have a girl who has low self-esteem, who won't eat and who cuts herself. Add what Graham did to her and it only confirms her opinion of herself: she's worthless, deserving of such a fate, therefore she isn't fit to be on this earth, she isn't fit to live.

'Her mother had no idea. In fact, the girl didn't mention it for several weeks and then only to her psychiatrist who couldn't be sure it wasn't one of her attention-seeking gambits or a paranoid delusion. She told him she had been raped. We don't think this was true but Malcolm Graham certainly did do something to her. The psychiatrist confirms her behaviour deteriorated at this stage but thinks she might have been speaking figuratively, that something had happened to her, something that was an invasion of her mind or person.'

'I think I'm losing track already.'

'Well, do you remember me telling you about another woman, the one who had her handbag stolen?'

'Yes. Then it was returned.'

'Well, that woman, Jane Stevenson, knew Elaine Pritchard, Anna's mother. They had met at the hospital. Jane had told her she went to the Coach and Horses every night after work, from five until five thirty. Elaine then told her family, only by way of conversation. Apparently she said she wished she could do something along the same lines. The family consists of a married sister with children and the mother, Sheila Foster.' Ian knew he was safe in telling Moira, that nothing he said went any further, not even after it was made public knowledge.

'Anna Pritchard didn't confide in her mother but she was very close to her grandmother. She did tell her.' It was another half an hour before Ian had finished the story.

Once Sheila Foster had been arrested she had volunteered to make a statement.

'There's no need for a formal interview,' she had said. 'I killed him. I can either tell you how or write it down for you.' She had spoken clearly, slowly and articulately while the tape recorder ran and Ian and Brenda listened.

'I had taken Anna shopping one day. We were in Brockham's when Anna's attitude suddenly changed. She became very subdued and anxious. A man was walking towards us, I had no idea who he was. "That's him," Anna said. "That's the man who photographed me." I had no idea what she was talking about but she was becoming hysterical so I hurried her out of the store.

'Much later, when she was calmer, she told me what had happened. She'd been sitting on the wall near the church when he pulled up in his car and offered her a lift. He said he'd seen her there before and that he knew her mother, which he didn't. Maybe his offices overlook the High Street, maybe he was lying.

'Anna accepted the lift. She'd absconded from home and realised her mother would be worried. They were going the wrong way. He stopped the car in an isolated spot and made her

169

get out. He started to undress her. She panicked, kicking and screaming, but he removed her pants and pushed her down. Apparently he did no more than take her picture and then he threatened to send it to her parents if she didn't keep quiet. He obviously had no idea about the sort of girl he was dealing with. Perhaps he thought that because she accepted the lift she was sexually experienced and knew what to expect – if not, that out of fear she'd go along with him. Anna told me she walked home and tried to cover herself by saying she'd thrown her underwear away. Despite her problems she knew how much Elaine worried about her and what it would do to her if she ever found out. Unfortunately Anna had no idea what it would eventually do to herself.

'I, too, protected Elaine from the truth, but Anna's condition deteriorated from then on. When she killed herself I decided I wanted revenge. It was premeditated and, I believed, well planned. I love my children deeply and I adore my grand-children but I had lost one of them. My loss was nothing compared to Elaine's, though.

'Around the time of the anniversary of Anna's death was the time I had in mind. I decided to hire a car. Not there, in Ipswich, but closer to where that animal lived. On the Friday I caught a train to Rickenham Green with the intention of walking up to Pender's Garage. I'd heard they were very reliable. However, the toilets at the station were locked because of vandalism and I needed to find one.

'You see, so very much of life is chance. Because I was in Rickenham and passing the Coach and Horses I remembered Elaine telling me about Jane Stevenson whom she had met at the hospital. I decided to buy an orange juice and use their amen-ities. Mrs Stevenson was there. At least, I was certain it had to be her. She was alone and fitted Elaine's description of her. "She's rather stately and she's got the greenest eyes I've ever seen," she told me. I almost spoke to her but at that moment she got up to go to the Ladies. She'd left her handbag on the seat. I was standing behind the back of the bench. It was easy to reach down and pick it up. No one noticed. Why should they? Most women carry handbags. That evening I only had a shopping bag, into which it fitted. I left quickly and without drawing attention to myself. I intended returning the handbag and its contents, which

170

I did. Only now do I see that I might have placed guilt on innocent shoulders, that Jane Stevenson could have become involved. If that young man at Pender's had not taken an interest in my daughter, Marion, none of this would have come to light.

'Of course, I immediately realised I couldn't use that woman's identity, I was too old. I instantly regretted what I had done until I realised there was someone who would help me without questions being asked. I rang Marion and asked her to meet me in Rickenham, but that she was to catch the bus. I gave her the handbag and asked her to hire a car for me using Jane Stevenson's name. She wouldn't do it at first. I explained there was no chance of anyone finding out and that it wasn't stealing, only borrowing. I begged her to trust me and then, I'm ashamed to admit, I used emotional blackmail. Yes, I implicated my daughter. But, you see, time was running out.

'I couldn't stand the thought that Elaine was actually working for that man, not that either of them knew of the connection with Anna. Also, I was aware that once you started your inquiries you would interview the staff at Brockham's. Once you were aware that I was Elaine's mother there was the slimmest chance you'd discover I'd hired a car if I used my own name.

'It had to be that weekend, my belated birthday dinner, because I could be sure Elaine would be at my house, that she had an alibi. Even then I had no idea how I would go about protecting Marion, although it would never have crossed her mind she had assisted me in such a matter. She is totally innocent.

'Once Marion had the car we drove to Saxborough where I dropped her, then I telephoned Malcolm Graham from a call box. The three of us sound exactly alike over the phone. He believed I was Elaine.

'Oh, I forgot to mention I had written to him, pointing out his fate. I don't know if you found my letters. Anyway, Elaine and Marion both have keys to my house. Elaine arrived, as arranged, and let herself in. I told her I had to do something and wouldn't be home until eight. As it happened it was later than that but she'd been very busy in the kitchen and I don't think she noticed just how late.

'I had told that vile man that I knew Sylvie Harris was fiddling

171

the books and that I had the proof. He agreed to see me at once. I parked in a gateway, walked over the field and found him in the garden. He had been expecting Elaine. I explained that she felt guilty, that she had sent me instead. He poured me a drink and one for himself into which I dropped some crushed barbiturates. He didn't taste them but he had been drinking already, I could smell it. It was so easy to get him upstairs, you wouldn't believe it. I said I'd show him the proof later. Once there I killed him and went home.'

'You mean she seduced him?' Moira asked, incredulous, when Ian had finished.

'It's more believable than you might think. Sheila Foster is a very glamorous woman, ten times better than Sylvie Harris who he also slept with. She said she thought Graham had been expecting a little recreation with Elaine and was therefore in the right mood.'

'But how did she actually do it?'

'They both got undressed. Naturally Graham would not have been suspicious, not with a naked woman in his bedroom. She told him to lie on the bed, which he did. She pulled the knife from her bag and stabbed him, telling him why she was doing so. She said that cutting off his penis was a way of making him suffer the indignity he had imposed on Anna and probably on others. She showered and dressed and left. And you know the rest.'

'But no fingerprints?'

'Nothing definite. And she didn't wash the glass she'd used, she simply toook it with her.'

'And the car? How did she get it back to Pender's?'

'Marion's family came on the Sunday. Marion's husband suggested she stay overnight again when Sheila complained of feeling unwell. She'd told us he was a very understanding man. Later I learned why. Once the family had gone Marion drove the car back and returned to her mother's on the bus.

'But, Ian, I still don't see how this Marion can be innocent. No one would do all that without knowing why.'

'I'll tell you why in a minute.'

'All right, then how did Marion know Jane Stevenson's mother lived in Saffron Walden?'

'No mystery there. Jane had mentioned it to Elaine during one

172

of their hospital visits. Elaine then told her sister because that was where Marion's husband came from and wondered if they had ever met.'

Moira nodded. People did pass on useless bits of information like that. If you found out that two people came from the same town you always asked if they knew one another. 'What happens now?'

'Jane Stevenson doesn't want to press charges over the stolen handbag and Roger Pender's in the clear. Marion, if she gets sentenced at all, will probably receive a suspended sentence.'

'And Sheila Foster?'

'Ah, well, this is where it all hinges. We couldn't understand two things, why Marion acted as she had done and how killing Malcolm Graham would have brought a sense of relief to Elaine. I asked Mrs Foster what good it would do Elaine.'

'She would've known – well, she does know now,' Sheila Foster had replied. 'You see, I wrote both my daughters a letter, to be opened in the event of my death.'

'But that might be twenty or thirty years away,' Ian had said.

Sheila Foster had literally thrown back her head and laughed. 'Oh, no, Chief Inspector, nowhere near that long.'

Ian drained his glass. 'Marion did as her mother requested as a last favour because she knew she was dying. She had said her son-in-law was understanding – that was because he, too, was aware of this. Marion knew but Elaine did not, they felt she had enough to cope with already. Mrs Foster intended telling her nearer the time, when she'd had a chance to get over her own loss. However, it turns out Elaine had guessed anyway.

'"I had nothing to lose," Sheila Foster told me. "Quite soon life itself will become a prison far worse than any you can send me to." That was her attitude. Her doctor has confirmed that her health is deteriorating rapidly, that there's very little chance of her appearing in court. She's signed a confession and says she cannot see the point of hiring a lawyer. I think now that she has achieved her end she'll give into her illness.'

'The poor woman. What a tragic family.' Moira stood up. It was time to distract Ian. 'Are you ready to eat?' The kitchen was warm from the heat of the oven. Moira opened the back door and began to lay the table.

'Yes. I'd just like to make one phone call first.'

Moira groaned. Was there no end to work?

In the hall Ian dialled Carmen Brockham's number. She answered almost immediately. He was surprised she was at home – he had intended leaving a message asking her to contact him.

'Oh, I thought it would be Neil.' She sounded both nervous and disappointed. 'I took your advice but he won't wait any longer for an answer. I said I'd let him know tonight.'

'Miss Brockham, we have arrested and charged someone with the murder of Malcolm Graham. It is highly unlikely that your name will be mentioned other than as his employer. I can safely say you can accept Mr Longman's proposal . . . Hello? Are you still there?'

The silence was broken by a sob. Carmen looked around for something with which to wipe her eyes. She had forgotten what it was to cry, and she had never cried with happiness. 'Thank you,' she said. 'Thank you so very much.'

A couple of minutes later Ian sat down to home-made watercress soup followed by a lamb and garlic casserole. All of a sudden he was starving and tomorrow was Sunday and he wasn't going in. Scruffy Short had said he would tidy up any loose ends before his lunchtime session in the pub which would be followed by a different sort of session with Nancy in the afternoon. Eddie Roberts would spend the day with his extended family and Alan Campbell would do whatever it was he did before he was officially back on duty. It's time he got a life for himself, Ian thought.

Brenda Gibbons would spend the day at the coast with Andrew. Ian hoped their happiness would last, Brenda deserved a break. And what of Mark? Would his marriage last when so many failed? Only time would tell. 'I think coffee and a brandy would round that off nicely,' Ian said, pushing his plate away. 'It was delicious.'

'I can't believe it, it really is all or nothing,' Ian said a fortnight later when he opened his post. He handed Moira a thick piece of card upon which was printed an invitation to the marriage of

Carmen Brockham to Neil Longman. 'It'll be a grand affair, I imagine, and the press'll be there.'

'I'll need a new dress,' Moira said with a smile.

'And you shall have one.' She deserved it, she was his source of stability, a refreshing change from what he dealt with at work. The psychiatric reports had come through. As they'd thought, Sheila Foster, knowing her time was limited, became obsessed with punishing the man who had so deeply harmed her family. She had had nothing to lose.

But they had also gained some insight into Malcolm Graham's character once it was discovered that his mother was still alive, looked after in a nursing home. Malcolm had kept no record of her address, nor had he been in contact with her for years.

'He hated women,' she said, 'me, especially. His father died when he was a small boy. I never remarried. Perhaps I should have done. Poor Diane. I made so many objections when Malcolm wanted to marry her, but they were for her own good. I knew he would use her as he used everyone. I was proved right.

'What he did, it doesn't surprise me. He was fixated – is that the word? – with sex. These young women would have made him feel like what he believed a man should feel like: powerful.'

'He didn't have sex with them,' Brenda had told her gently when she visited the home.

'Oh, no, he wouldn't have. He probably didn't have it in him.'

'But there were a couple of women who were almost his contemporaries.'

'Yes, and I can imagine how he treated them. Like dirt, the way he always treated me. Miss Gibbons, my son was never right. Nowadays I expect he'd have seen a child psychologist but discipline was the only answer then and I failed to exercise it once he was no longer a small boy. I'm ashamed to admit I was frightened of him.' She smiled sadly. 'How odd that I should outlive him.' She paused. 'I suppose being the manager of Brockham's made him feel powerful, too. Well, we'll never know now how his mind worked but at least he can't bother young women any longer.'

Brenda had only gone to break the news. She had not expected so much information. Ian listened to what she had heard and wondered just how many more women out there had been subjected to the man's tyranny.

Shortly after the wedding Sheila Foster died. She had been released on bail on the condition she stayed with one of her daughters, awaiting sentencing. A duty solicitor had acted on her behalf. Both her daughters had been with her at the end. 'She just gave up,' Elaine Pritchard told Ian. 'She had nothing left to live for. She was as obsessed as he was. I'm just glad she spent her last weeks in hospital and not prison.'

'So am I,' Ian told her. 'So am I.' And, murderess or not, he meant it.